Lost in Ireland

WITHDRAWN

Also by Cindy Callaghan

Just Add Magic

Lost in London

Lost in Paris

Lost in Rome

WITHDRAWN

Lost in Ireland

CINDY CALLAGHAN

Previously titled *Lucky Me*

Aladdin M!X
New York   London   Toronto   Sydney   New Delhi

If you purchased this book without a cover, you should be aware that this book is stolen property. It was reported as "unsold and destroyed" to the publisher, and neither the author nor the publisher has received any payment for this "stripped book."

This book is a work of fiction. Any references to historical events, real people, or real places are used fictitiously. Other names, characters, places, and events are products of the author's imagination, and any resemblance to actual events or places or persons, living or dead, is entirely coincidental.

m!x

ALADDIN M!X
Simon & Schuster Children's Publishing Division
1230 Avenue of the Americas, New York, NY 10020
First Aladdin M!X edition March 2016
Text copyright © 2014 by Cindy Callaghan
Previously titled *Lucky Me*
Cover illustration copyright © 2016 by Annabelle Metayer
Also available in an Aladdin hardcover edition.
All rights reserved, including the right of reproduction
in whole or in part in any form.
ALADDIN is a trademark of Simon & Schuster, Inc.,
and related logo is a registered trademark of Simon & Schuster, Inc.
ALADDIN M!X and related logo are registered trademarks of Simon & Schuster, Inc.
For information about special discounts for bulk purchases,
please contact Simon & Schuster Special Sales at 1-866-506-1949 or
business@simonandschuster.com.
The Simon & Schuster Speakers Bureau can bring authors to your
live event. For more information or to book an event contact the
Simon & Schuster Speakers Bureau at 1-866-248-3049 or
visit our website at www.simonspeakers.com.
Series designed by Jessica Handelman
Cover designed by Karina Granda
Interior designed by Hilary Zarycky
The text of this book was set in Goudy Oldstyle Std.
Manufactured in the United States of America 0116 OFF
2 4 6 8 10 9 7 5 3 1
Library of Congress Control Number 2015956190
ISBN 978-1-4814-6207-5 (hc)
ISBN 978-1-4814-6206-8 (pbk)
ISBN 978-1-4814-6208-2 (eBook)

To both of the Genes I've been lucky
to have known and loved.

Acknowledgments

I am one lucky girl to have so many wonderful people in my life to thank.

As always, I need to thank my ever faithful critique partners, the WIPs: Gale, Carolee, Josette, Jane, Chris, and Shannon, and the Northern Delaware Sisters in Crime group: John, KB, Jane, June, Chris, Janis, Susan, and Kathleen. I could write without them, but nothing would be very good.

Special thanks as always to my family: Ellie, Evan, Happy, Kevin, my parents, my nieces and nephews, my sister, my sisters-in-law, my brothers-in-law, and my mother-in-law.

Thanks to inspiring friends near and far, old and new.

I am the luckiest of lucksters to work with a literary dream team: Mandy Hubbard, literary agent, and Alyson Heller, editor. Without their help and support, none of this works.

To teachers and librarians. Most of all, to my readers—I love getting your e-mails, letters, pictures, selfies, posts, and Tweets . . . keep 'em coming! I hope you love *Lucky Me* as much as *Lost in London* and *Just Add Magic*.

To all of you above, and those I've somehow forgotten, I wish you luck in both your dreams and your realities.

Lost in Ireland

1

If I had to pick one thing that I believe in more than anything else, it would be this: LUCK. I'm Meghan McGlinchey, the most superstitious thirteen-year-old girl in Delaware, and possibly the world.

For example, I never got out of bed when my digital clock read an odd number. Odd number = bad luck.

7:02. Perfect.

I dressed in a snap because every day it was the same school uniform—boring plaid skirt, plain white shirt, itchy button-up navy-blue sweater, matching headband, horrendous blue leather shoes, and kneesocks. The outfit was—how should I say this?—ugly!

I dashed down the stairs, especially careful to skip

the thirteenth step today because it was a very important day, one I'd been looking forward to for weeks. I was running for eighth-grade class president. And today was the election. I had done a stellar job campaigning FOREVER. If I didn't totally mess up my speech, I was pretty sure I was gonna win. With all the practicing I'd been doing, it would take a major freak of nature for me to mess it up.

I passed my four sisters and parents scrambling around in the kitchen. I opened a can of food for my cat, Lucky. He ran over when he heard it pop. I scratched his ears as he lapped up the food.

I loved Lucky, but he and I had a problem. He was a black cat. And people like me, we didn't mix well with black cats. But we had an understanding: He didn't cross my path, and I took good care of him. It worked for us.

The kitchen was louder than usual this morning. My younger sister Piper (the fifth grader) yelled at one of my older sisters, Eryn (the eleventh grader), "Why did you touch my playlist? Why? WHY?"

Dad yelled across the kitchen to my mom, "Can you put a bagel in the toaster for me?"

The baby, Hope, cried while my oldest sister sang her

an Irish lullaby to calm her. It wasn't working, so she tried some applesauce, which the baby threw across the room. It nearly hit my white shirt, but I ducked out of the way just in time. *SPLAT!* The applesauce hit the wall behind me.

Phew, that was lucky!

I stood at the front door, under the horseshoe mounted on the wall and next to my snow globe collection, watching the insanity.

The living room was a mess with suitcases and duffel bags. We were leaving the next morning for Ireland, where we would spend spring break. The purpose of the trip was for my father to meet his newly discovered sister. You see, he'd been born in Ireland. Sadly, something happened to his parents when he was just a kid, and he'd been raised at a home for boys.

Until a few months ago he hadn't thought he had any family. But thanks to some online research, he'd found a long-lost sister. I imagined that when he met her, he'd introduce me as his middle daughter and president of Wilmington Prep's eighth-grade class. It was gonna be totally impressive.

I crunched the granola bar I'd packed in my back-pack the night before—instant breakfast. With a little planning, my morning was the way I liked it: mayhem-free.

In fact, I liked most things organized. I might have been the most organized eighth grader at Wilmington Prep, an all-girls private school that went from kindergarten through twelfth grade. This meant that Piper and Eryn were in my school. If you knew either Piper or Eryn, you'd know this wasn't a good thing. (Piper was known as the bigmouth, while Eryn was quiet and filled with a bad attitude. I'd heard a lot of nicknames for her, most made up by my bestie, Carissa. None of them were nice.)

While I waited for someone to realize it was time to leave, I flipped through a Forever 21 catalog.

"Meghan," Mom called through the chaos. "You have a letter on the table."

"A letter?" I asked.

"Yes," she said. "You know, the regular old-fashioned paper kind that's delivered by a mailman."

I stepped around the chaos. Sure enough, on the hall table was a letter addressed to *moi*.

Who writes letters anymore when you can just text or e-mail? The postmark on the envelope said Limerick, Ireland. *Hmmm.*

Dear Friend,

I am starting this chain letter and mailing it to three people to whom I would like to send good luck. In turn they must send it to three people. If you are receiving this, someone has sent the luck to you—as long as you, in turn, send it to three more people within six days.

Chain letters have existed for centuries, and many have traveled around the world. A United States police officer received $25,000 within one day of sending his letters. However, another woman ignored it and lost her life's fortune because she broke the chain. A Norwegian fisherman thought for sure he would never find true love, but just two days after sending his letters, he met the woman of his dreams.

To get your luck and avoid the unlucky consequences, you must:

- Copy this letter
- Add your name below and remove the name above yours
- Mail it to three people within <u>six</u> days

From,

4. <u>Clare Gallagher, Ireland</u>

5. _____

Clare Gallagher?

I didn't know anyone by that name. *How does she know me?* That wasn't important now. What *was* important was that I send this letter to three people ASAP. No, double-ASAP. Maybe I could get the good luck as soon as today—for the election—and avoid those "unlucky consequences."

I went into my mom and dad's home office and rummaged around.

"What are you doing in there?" Mom called over the havoc.

"Looking for envelopes!"

"I don't have any," Mom said. "Sorry. I'll bring a few home from work tonight."

That would be too late. Maybe I could get a couple from the school office. I only needed three. "How about stamps?"

"Sorry. The baby used them as stickers. I can buy more after vacation."

After vacation wasn't *today*, and I needed the luck *today*.

Eryn bumped me out of her way, causing me to drop the letter. "Move it, buttmunch," she said. She stepped on the letter as she left the house. (This is what I meant about her attitude—bad.)

Piper did pretty much the same thing on her way out, not because she had attitude issues but because she wasn't paying attention.

Shannon picked the letter up for me. She was twenty-two years old and definitely the nicest of my sisters. She commuted to the University of Delaware, and itched to finish school so she could move out of our house and "find herself," whatever that meant.

I took the letter, followed Shannon to the car, and climbed into the back with Piper. Eryn sat shotgun. Always. I didn't even try to beat her to the front seat anymore. Shannon always dropped us off at Wilmington Prep, then headed to UD. She picked us up later, on her way home. After school, we did homework or whatever until Mom or Dad got home from the law firm where they worked together. They were always home for a late full-family dinner, when we talked about our day, whether we wanted to or not.

On our drive Piper chattered about our spring break trip, while I just stared out the window.

"What do you guys know about chain letters?" I asked.

Shannon said, "You need to send 'em right away, don't you?"

I could feel Eryn rolling her eyes.

Piper asked a hundred questions: "What's a chain letter? . . . Who sent it? . . . Why? Can you send it back? . . . Why not? How come I didn't get one? . . . Huh?"

I didn't answer her; I responded to Shannon. "I don't have any stamps or envelopes, and I want the good luck today."

"Why don't you e-mail it?" Shannon asked. "You could do that right now on your phone."

Piper said, "Problem solved. Shannon is supersmart. . . ." She continued to ramble on while I typed the letter quickly with my thumbs. I reread it to make sure I hadn't made any mistakes. I put my name on the bottom and didn't put Clare's. When I finished, Piper was still talking. "She gets As in college. That's a lot of hard work."

I hit the send button on my phone, and e-mail chain letters went out to three friends from summer camp. "Okay. It's done. Let the good luck begin!"

Eryn snickered.

"What?" I asked.

"Oh, nothing," she said with a smirk. "Let me know how that works for you. On second thought, don't. That would mean you'd be talking to me." She made a grossed-out face that I caught in the side mirror. "But any moron knows that you can't e-mail a snail-mail chain letter. It's cheating. And chain letters have a way of messing with cheaters."

Piper said, "Uh-oh."

Uh-oh?

I couldn't have any *uh-oh.*

Not today.

2

As soon as I walked into science class, it looked like Eryn might have been right. "Miss McGlinchey," Ms. Geneva called to me. "Please report to the front of the classroom for a demerit."

A *demerit?* I didn't get demerits. I followed all the rules all the time, to avoid getting demerits. I followed the rules even when demerits *weren't* involved. I flossed, waited twenty minutes after eating to swim, and wore SPF 50 sunscreen every day.

I took the yellow paper from her hand. For each demerit you got, you missed one recess. If you got five, you were suspended from school for a day. Ms. Geneva must have read the puzzled look on my face. She gestured toward my feet. "Your socks."

I looked down. One black, one blue.

OMG! Somehow, for the first time in my history of wearing kneesocks, I had accidentally mismatched them. *But that could happen to anyone, right?*

I sulked all the way back to my desk.

"What the heck?" Carissa looked shocked as I sat back down.

"My stupid socks don't match," I grumbled.

Carissa chuckled. "You can hardly tell," she said a little bit too loudly.

"Shh," I said. "Or you'll get one too."

"Oh, like that would be something new. You know they named a desk after me in detention. Not many people can claim that." Carissa missed a lot of recesses, and she'd been suspended twice. On those days, she said she'd sat on the couch all day eating popcorn and watching on-demand movies—R-rated. Her mom was home way more than mine but never had a clue what Carissa did. Carissa's life was kinda the opposite of mine.

The teacher said, "*Mademoiselle Carissa Lyons, fermez la bouche!*" Everyone has to take French as part of Wilmington Prep's curriculum, so we both knew that was a teacher's polite way of saying "Shut up."

. . .

Considering all the preparation I'd done, I was way more nervous for my speech than I should've been. I sat on the stage, in mismatched socks, in front of the entire eighth-grade class. This speech would seal the election for me. I'd worked hard on it, and it was—how can I say this so that it doesn't sound like I'm bragging?—perfect! I had nothing to worry about.

I imagined the scene as though it was frozen in one of my lucky snow globes: I'm on stage delivering my last sentence, but before I finish, the room booms with applause. Kids stand up and cheer. My opponent is so intimidated, she walks offstage—she doesn't stand a chance. She knows it. I know it.

The principal introduced me and my opponent, Avery Brown, and she explained that we each had four minutes.

I was up first. I stepped to the podium and began:

"Fellow classmates," I started confidently, "my name is Meghan McGlinchey. I want to be your class president for three very important reasons. First, I am filled with Wilmington Prep school spirit. . . ."

I looked into the crowd and noticed that everyone was talking to each other like I wasn't even there.

I held up two fingers. "Secondly." Still the crowd talked among themselves. I could hear them like a rumble. Why weren't they listening to my amazing speech? I was being very clear, articulate, and was holding up fingers.

Principal Jackson came out from behind the stage's curtain and walked over to the podium, where I was already talking about point number three and holding up three fingers.

"Excuse me," she whispered, interrupting my flow.

I whispered back to her, "What's the matter?"

"The microphone—" She flipped a switch with her thumb, and her words bellowed: "IT ISN'T TURNED ON!" She moved it away from her mouth. "It is now."

My fellow classmates laughed.

They hadn't heard a single perfect word I'd said. I started over. "My name is—"

The girl who was keeping time in the front row said, "One minute."

One minute?

"Reason number one . . ." I raced.

"Number two . . ." I spoke faster, threw up two fingers.

"And number three—"

"Time!" the timekeeper said.

Principal Jackson walked out clapping her hands. "Thank you, Meghan."

"B-but," I sputtered. "The mic."

"Very good job. Next we have Avery Brown."

I passed Avery as I went back to my chair and she approached the podium. She said, "Bad luck for you."

It was.

What have I done?

3

The election was during lunch in the school courtyard. I stood near the ballot box, ready to shake hands with my fellow eighth-grade voters. My hands were sweaty.

Carissa entered the courtyard covered in VOTE FOR MEGHAN buttons.

"Did you hear that speech?" I asked her.

"I couldn't hear much."

"Thanks a lot," I said.

"Just being honest. It wasn't great," she admitted. "But we can't go back and change it. You're gonna have to win this election *right now*."

The spring breeze picked up. It was cool and felt good.

"I am?"

"Yes. Ready?"

I nodded.

Loudly Carissa asked me, "So, what do you plan to do about our aging technology in the computer lab, Candidate Meghan McGlinchey?"

She knew I had a good answer to this. "A car wash!" I said, loud enough for everyone to hear. "We'll have a car wash in the parking lot during the statewide track meet that Wilmington Prep is hosting. Over two thousand cars will pass through here that day."

"That's an incredible idea," Carissa said. "It sounds like a lot of fun, too!" Some of my classmates seemed to perk up at the idea, but it started to get colder in the courtyard, and they slowly migrated inside. Carissa tried to keep the voters in the area by yelling, "What about cafeteria food? Who's concerned about the quality of our cafeteria food?"

"I am!" I said, and I detailed my plan.

I could hear some of the girls who were waiting in line to cast their vote say how excited they were about my idea for a student cooking contest in the cafeteria to improve the food. It was something I'd read about in an ebook.

Carissa was brilliant. Heck, *I* was brilliant! Maybe

everyone in line voted for me before they ran inside to get out of the cold wind.

Things were looking good, until a big gust of wind knocked over the ballot box. Papers—all of the ballots—scattered *everywhere*.

4

In between the election and our monthly school assembly—a magic show by the Fabulous Frank-O—Carissa asked, "What's with you today?"

I quickly explained the snail-mail–e-mail chain letter conundrum and showed Carissa the letter. She instantly pulled me into a nearby restroom and into a stall.

"What are we doing here? Whatever it is, I don't think it'll cheer me up," I complained.

She took out her state-of-the-art—and strictly off-limits during school—phone. I'd put mine in a cubby when I'd walked into school, just like we were supposed to. Carissa never did.

"Are you kidding me?" I asked. "You're holding enough

demerits in your hand to get us both expelled." I started to shake in my mismatched socks.

"Rules, rules. You're always about rules. Let's think of the cell phone rule more as *un conseil*, or a guideline. I mean, what if there was an emergency? *This* is an emergency. You're lucky you have me to help you put things into perspective."

"I'm feeling anything but lucky today. In fact, I feel like any minute the sky might fall right onto my head."

"Don't pull a Chicken Little on me just yet." She touched the phone's screen. I would've paced around if I could, but it was cramped in the stall, which was a gross place for our rendezvous.

"Don't worry. This thing is faster than lightning," Carissa said. "It's got, like, six or eight Gs. Gimme two secs, and I'll figure out the official way you can reverse the bad luck of a snail-mail–e-mail chain letter sitch."

"How are you going to do that?"

"A little invention called Google." She read the screen. "Uh-huh . . . uh-huh . . . uh-huh."

I asked, "What is it?"

"Easy peasy. You just have to find the people—the links—before you on the letter and ask them to forgive you for e-mailing your letter. If-slash-when they agree, you do a double-handed handshake. *Pas de problème.*"

"Can I just call them? Or e-mail them?" I asked. "That would be a lot easier and faster."

"If you can figure out how to shake hands over the phone or Internet, that would be a magic trick worthy of the Fab Frank-O."

"What's a double-handed handshake?" I asked.

She held the phone between her knees. "Like this." She crossed her arms and reached for my hands, shaking both of my hands at the same time. "You could add a hip bump like this, if you wanted to shake things up." She swung her hip into mine—a little too hard, because I banged into the metal toilet paper holder.

"Okay, so hand-shaking the links might be easy if chain letters didn't travel around the world for hundreds of years. That makes it pretty tough to find the senders, considering they've probably been dead and buried for a long time," I said, rubbing my hip where it had hit the holder.

She took the letter from me. "See, you *are* lucky, because you have *moi.* I'm way more attentive to details than you are when you're an emotional wreck due to crazy socks." She took the folded-up letter out of my fist and pointed to the name on the letter. "See here that Clare is link number four. And you're number five? This is a brand-spanking-new chain letter. That might be a problem for some unlucky suckers, but you're going to Ireland tomorrow."

Carissa was right. Only four links in this shiny new chain.

We stepped out of the cramped bathroom stall and walked right into the ample gut of Mrs. Swarez-Vincent, whose hand was extended for Carissa's phone. Carissa placed the phone into Mrs. S-V's outstretched palm, and it disappeared inside a sea of polyester pants. Mrs. S-V's hand reemerged with two demerit slips. We didn't argue.

With yellow papers and flushed cheeks, we walked to the auditorium for the assembly. Carissa didn't seem nearly as angry as I was. The yellow paper didn't upset her, and she'd probably have another cell phone before dinner tonight. I, on the other hand, would be haunted by guilt for hours—if not days. I'd made it to my eighth-grade year without a single demerit, and now I'd gotten two in one morning!

All because of that STUPID letter.

5

I took a seat in the back of the auditorium, trying to keep a low profile. The Fabulous Frank-O ran out to center stage under a majestic purple cloak, trying to give the illusion he was flying. From the "oohs" and "aahs," I could tell the little kids bought it. It didn't take me long to figure out I was way too old for this gig.

I picked at my cuticles and watched Frank-O out of the corner of my eye. He pointed his index fingers at his temples. "I need a volunteer." He squeezed his eyes shut. "Is there a Hayden Posey in the audience?"

Hayden was friends with Piper and would have loved to be chosen as a volunteer. I looked for her to leap onto the stage, but no Hayden. Guess she'd picked today to stay home sick.

Frank-O peeked an eye open, and when he saw that no one was approaching the stage, he squeezed his eyes shut again. "How about Meg . . . Meghan McDonal . . . no . . . McGlinchey?"

"No way." I sank low in my seat, hoping he would just choose another name.

I heard Piper yell, "That's my sister! She's here! Meghan, THAT'S YOU!"

"Go." Carissa nudged me.

"I don't wanna."

"Oh, come on," she said. "Go along with it. It'll be fun. It's for the kids. It's very presidential."

"Fine." I got up and walked to the stage with my head down. My face flushed as I went up the steps to meet Frank-O. He moved his hands from his head and held them out for me. They were clammy. From close up I could see he was older than I'd originally thought.

"You look like the perfect victim—ha-ha, I mean *volunteer*, of course—to be cut in half."

Cut in half?

I felt sick. Puking on stage was a real possibility. *That* wouldn't be very presidential. The way my luck was going today, I wouldn't have legs in a few minutes.

Frank-O swooped to the side of the stage and rolled out a case that looked kinda like a coffin on a table. It had a hole at each end—one for my head and one for my feet.

Frank-O lifted the case's wooden lid. With a sigh I started to climb in. "Wait," he said. "Please take off your shoes and socks." He did a double take when he saw my socks. Using a step stool, I climbed into the box. Frank-O clicked a latch that locked me in. He held up a mirror to show me that my body was, in fact, closed in the box. From this angle my feet looked like a caveman's. The Fabulous Frank-O spoke with dramatic flair, "This will only hurt for a second." The elementary kids giggled.

Frank-O pulled and pushed a fierce-looking saw.

My heart raced. The blade moved lower and lower. I closed my eyes and wiggled.

I guess I wiggled a little too much, because the coffin rolled off the table, crashed onto the stage, and broke open, revealing to everyone that the caveman feet were *fake*! As I lay on the stage I could see an arched slot through which the scary saw was bent—it was made of rubber!

The older kids laughed while the younger ones' mouths flew open. The little kids whispered to each other in confusion.

"It's not real magic?"

"He isn't really a magician?"

A smattering of "boos" came up from the crowd.

Frank-O sneered at me and let out a low growl. Then he smiled to the crowd and waved his purple-cloaked arms around. The crowd didn't give in. To distract them Frank-O stuck a finger into his mouth and pulled out the corner of a scarf, and pulled and pulled and pulled a long row of scarves, all from his mouth.

No one seemed to care whether I was okay after falling off a table in a coffin. I slid my socks back on—one black, one blue. I stood to return to my seat, with my shoes in hand. But because I was wearing only my socks, the stage was superslippery. And I slid. Right into Fab Frank-O, who fell on his magician's butt, spilling magic coins, cards, and handcuffs from his pockets. A little pod, which he'd scrunched in his mouth, flew out.

No magic. Just tricks.

I offered him my hand to get up, but he didn't take it. I carefully slid on my feet, like I was wearing ice skates, off the stage and walked to my seat in the back of the auditorium. On my way by, a second grader said to me, "You ruined everything."

Her friend added, "You stink, Meghan McGlinchey!"

I was mad, embarrassed, and, well, having a really bad day, so I yelled back at her. "You stink worse, and there's no such thing as magic, stupid!"

The little girls said nothing. They looked over my shoulder at what turned out to be Mrs. S-V.

"My office," she said to me.

I slipped on my super-duper ugly shoes and ran down the aisle, getting nasty looks from every girl under the age of eleven for whom I'd just ruined the Fabulous Frank-O show. Tears streamed down my cheeks. *I didn't want to be a volunteer.*

Eventually, I was in a chair in Mrs. S-V's office, which, thankfully, was supplied with tissues. I used a lot of them while thinking about my impending expulsion.

I wondered if I'd ever be allowed to attend an assembly again. Maybe if I could explain that this wasn't my fault, it was the chain letter, Mrs. S-V would understand. Probably not. She didn't really seem like the understanding type.

She left me waiting for a long time. My stomach growled; it hadn't gotten any lunch today. When Mrs. S-V finally arrived, she didn't yell at me like I'd expected. She gave me three more demerits for calling second graders stupid and left me in her office for the remainder of the day.

26

That was *cinq* demerits, which equaled one day's suspension for unlucky Meghan McGlinchey.

From the hard wooden seat in Mrs. S-V's office, I heard the school's sound system click on.

"Good afternoon, students," Principal Jackson's voice bellowed. "I am pleased to announce the results of the eighth-grade election. The new president is . . ."

I crossed my fingers, arms, and legs. If I'd been at my locker, I would have also palmed my lucky rabbit's foot and stood under the horseshoe that hung on the inside. *Please say "Meghan McGlinchey." Please say "Meghan McGlinchey."*

"Avery Brown."

What?

I'd lost.

There was no way.

I thought for sure everyone had walked up and put my name in the ballot box.

How can this be happening?

I knew exactly how.

I'd cheated a chain letter, and now I was—how can I put this delicately?—cursed!

6

When I finally came out of school, Carissa was waiting for me, leaning against the brick wall. She tossed me my backpack.

"Did you hear that announcement?" I asked.

"I heard it, but I don't believe it," Carissa said. "Do you want to protest? Demand a recount? Because I'll do it. Something smells fishy."

"No. I just want to go to Ireland and forget it ever happened."

"That Frank-O scene should help you forget about the election. It was *très* epic. People will be talking about it for years, decades maybe." She unwrapped a pack of gum and held a piece out for me.

I shook my head.

"Come on. School's over. It's okay now."

I took it, but I didn't unwrap it until I was outside the front gates, where Shannon would pick up me, Piper, and Eryn, but they weren't there.

"Shannon was already here," Carissa said. "Bigmouth Piper told her everything. She's waiting across the street at the Donut Hole." Then, out of the corner of her mouth she said, "You and I both know there's way better stuff at the Hole than doughnuts." She was referring to the boys from Chesapeake Academy. They hung out there and played the store's video games. Carissa added, "Come on. We'll get your mind off the election *and* the assembly. Carbs, sugar, and Chesapeake boys will help. I promise."

"Is Shannon bringing you home today?"

Carissa often caught a ride home because she was way too cool for the bus, and she preferred hanging out with the dysfunctional McGlinchey girls to being in her house.

"You know it. She likes my company."

Shannon didn't particularly care for Carissa or her company.

Once we were across the street, I put the gum into my mouth. We walked through a small playground, where

I hopped over the hopscotch board: two, one, two, one, one, two. I hopped the board every time we cut through there, and now, to skip it would be unlucky. "Wait," I said to Carissa. I went back and hopped over the painted boxes again.

"What was that for?"

"I figured I could use a little extra oomph today, and for some reason that hopscotch board always gives me a good feeling."

"Maybe you should draw one on your driveway. That way you can do it every day," she suggested.

Carissa wasn't superstitious the way I was, but she tried to be supportive. For example, if she found a heads-up penny, she'd give it to me. That was the kind of friend she was.

Shannon was waiting for us outside. Carissa started for the door to the Hole, but Shannon called to her, "We already got some."

Carissa's back slumped at the idea of missing the boys from Chesapeake, and she got into the car.

At least the doughnuts smelled good.

"You know," Carissa said, pouting, "my future husband could be in there right now eating a Boston cream and waiting for me. He'll never meet me. Poor guy."

"Just buckle up." Shannon tossed her a bag with two chocolate glazed doughnuts.

Eryn texted silently in the front seat, probably to one of her equally angry friends.

The ride home was miserable.

Shannon asked, "What happened with the election?"

"I don't get it," I said. "I really thought everyone was putting my name in the ballot box."

"I want to protest. But she won't let me," Carissa added.

As if I didn't feel bad enough, Piper, who sat between Carissa and me, spoke over Shannon, telling the Frank-O story over and over, louder each time. "And then the coffin crashed to the ground. It dented the wood stage. You know they'll have to repair it?" In the next version they had to replace a section, and in the next they had to rebuild the whole stage.

Carissa tried to change the subject to get the heat off me. "How about them Yankees?"

But Piper said, "Wait till Mom finds out about the suspension."

"What?" Shannon shrieked.

Eryn laughed a little.

"Look, I had a really bad day. And actually it's *your* fault," I said to Shannon angrily.

"*My* fault? How did I get you in all that trouble?"

"I e-mailed that letter, which *you* told me to do, and now *I'm* cursed. Thank you very much."

Eryn spoke three words, "Told. You. So."

Piper asked, "What are you gonna do? You have to do something. Look at your socks!"

"According to Google," I explained, "if I find the links of the chain and ask them to forgive me, I can undo the curse."

Shannon said, "Then get on the phone, talk to the links, and undo the curse."

"There are a few complications," I said. "Apparently, I need to shake on it."

"What?" Shannon asked. "That doesn't make sense. I've never heard of this."

Carissa said, "Um . . . we found it online today. It was a new amendment to the chain letter rules. From 2011, I think. There was a convention or conclave or something."

"Another complication is that I don't know Clare Gallagher," I said.

"Hold on!" Piper exclaimed. "I know that name! Gallagher is one of the family people we're gonna see in Ireland. I've heard Dad say that name." She gasped. "I know what you can do! You can ask Clare where to find the person who sent *her* the letter. This is a good idea I'm having. Then meet *that* person and ask *them* where to find the person who sent them the letter. Then meet that person and ask *them*—"

I interrupted, "I get it."

Shannon said, "It isn't a terrible idea."

"Did you know we're staying at the Ballymore Home for Boys, where Dad grew up?" Piper asked. "We might be the first girls they've ever seen."

"A home for boys?" Carissa asked. "Now, that sounds like my kind of place."

Shannon sighed. "A home for *orphaned* boys."

"Oh, joy," Eryn said sarcastically. "We get to stay with a group of homeless kids. They sound like a blast!"

"They're hosting this year's Spring Fling event, where Dad will finally meet his long-lost sister," Shannon said.

Piper chimed in, "*That's* Gallagher. It's the lost sister. She must've sent you the letter."

Maybe this could work. Provided that I made it to

Ireland alive, I could meet Clare at the Spring Fling and get leads on the other links. I'd shake as many hands as they had. I'd shake their feet, if I had to.

I was going to reverse this curse!

I couldn't have another day like today. Not ever.

7

I watched the clouds over the Atlantic Ocean and rubbed my fingers over the silver four-leaf clover around my neck. In the seat next to me, Piper talked to the flight attendants whenever they came by, and she pushed the call button when she had something she wanted to say and they weren't around. My mom told her to stop a hundred times, but she didn't.

I ignored her and dozed off, until I woke up somewhere over County Cork, Ireland. From the view out my tiny plane window, it looked like the land was covered by plush, green vegetation. It also looked rainy, which wasn't going to be kind to my flat-ironed hair.

But I had a good feeling that my luck would get better once I was officially in Ireland.

After exiting the plane, I knew that feeling was totally wrong.

First the rain frizzed my hair.

Then our luggage was lost—all of it—even the new stuff from Delia's that I'd just bought for this trip.

Lastly, our ride that was taking us to Ballymore was late.

And then the big whopper happened. I saw a coin on the ground and bent to check if it was heads up. Eryn walked right into me, glued to her phone, and knocked me into Shannon, who I bumped down the escalator. Not on purpose, of course, but still, I watched helplessly as she tumbled down the moving stairs.

CRACK!

Shannon grabbed her leg and yelled in pain.

I ran down the steps to her side. "Where does it hurt?" I asked.

She pointed to her knee, shin, and ankle. *That can't be good*, I thought. I looked carefully at her leg. "It looks fine," I lied. Actually, her calf looked sort of, *well* . . . It was crooked where it shouldn't have been.

My mom took one look at her leg and went deathly white.

Dad took the baby from Mom and handed her to Eryn, who held Hope out at arm's length. "It's all going to be fine," he said.

A security guard ran over, pushed a button on the walkie-talkie Velcroed to his shoulder, and mumbled something in a thick Irish accent and told us, "Help's on the way."

"Help's on the way!" Piper repeated. "Did you hear that? *Help's* on the way. Help's *on the way*. Help—"

"We get it, buttmunch," Eryn said. "If you don't shut up, we'll have them take you to a place where you'll be locked up in a straitjacket."

"Mooooooom! Did you hear that? See what she does?"

Mom said, "Eryn, please." Tears rolled down her cheeks.

Eryn said, "Just for the week. Or two." She walked away from the chaos, still holding the baby away from her body, like embracing her might get vomit on her black denim jacket.

An ambulance arrived. Shannon was put on a stretcher and lifted into the back.

The baby cried, and Eryn passed her back to Mom.

"I'll go to the hospital," Dad said. "You take the baby straight to Ballymore?"

Mom asked, "What about our stuff? I only have one small bottle of formula left. We need our bags."

"Okay." Dad thought some more. "I'll stay here and fill out the reports. You go to the hospital, and Eryn can take Hope to Ballymore."

"I don't think so," Eryn said, horrified. "I really don't do babies."

"She's your sister," Mom snapped. "Make an exception."

The ambulance guy was ready to close the back doors. "We're heading out," he said.

Shannon sat up, wincing. "Just send Meghan with me."

"Okay," Dad agreed. "I'll get things sorted out here."

With that, I was popped into the back of the ambulance. We took off with a jolt. It felt like we were on a fast and wild carnival ride. Did I mention we were on the WRONG SIDE OF THE ROAD?

The stretcher rolled to one side of the small ambulance, bumped the metal wall, and rolled back over to me. It banged into my legs. "Ouch!" I complained as I rubbed them. Shannon shot me a look. After that I held the gurney as still as I could until I saw the County Cork Hospital emergency room sign.

A team of nurses took Shannon away. I sat and waited,

and waited. I felt terrible that I was the reason Shannon was there. I looked at my watch. It was four thirty a.m. at home.

I texted Carissa about our fiasco.

She wrote back right away like she was sleeping with her cell phone—which she probably was. Her text said, "That sux. Sit tight. On my way."

I chuckled at her funny reply before moping again. I figured we'd be on the next plane back to Delaware, where Shannon could see a surgeon and I'd be cursed for the rest of my life. I'd be banned from all magic shows, and would probably need to change schools.

Finally a nurse came out to get me.

I rushed to Shannon's side. Her leg was in a cast from her foot to just above her knee. "Are you okay?"

"I'm fine. I can't walk for a few days until I get a boot, but I'll be fine."

"I'm so sorry. This is all my fault. What am I going to do? Mom and Dad are going to make us all go home now, and I'll never find the links to that letter, and the rest of my life is going to be awful like this," I said, pointing at her leg.

"I believe you," Shannon said. "I admit I thought you were exaggerating about the socks, the magic show, and the election. But after the luggage, my leg, and . . ."

"What?" I asked.

"You should see your hair right now."

My hands flew to my head. Total frizz.

She touched my hand. "You might really be cursed. You should find the links before someone else gets hurt. I called Mom and told her everything was fine. We're not flying home. Dad is still looking for our luggage, and people at Ballymore are sending someone to pick us up."

I glanced at her superbig cast. "Are you really fine?"

"Just between you and me, I might need a small procedure when we get home. But no one needs to know that this week."

"You lied to Mom and Dad?"

"It's more like leaving out a tiny detail. It doesn't count." Shannon winked. "Go look for our escort."

I went back out to the waiting room and looked for a guy who looked like he was looking for us, although I wasn't sure what that would look like. The person who approached me was tall, lean, blond, and seemed only a year or two older than me, and he was—how should I say this?—supercute!

"Miss McGlinchey?"

"*Oui*—I mean *sí*—I mean yes. I'm Meghan." I was suddenly aware that I was still in the clothes I'd worn on the plane. I was tired, had frizzy bed head, and my breath smelled like—what would be a good word for it? I know—YUCK!

"I'm Finn. Welcome to County Cork, Miss Meghan. I hope you're finding it likable," he said with an Irish brogue that was adorable

"Very much, yes. I like it very much. Very much." Going to an all-girls school hadn't prepared me well to interact with boys my age. I watched Carissa talk to boys at the Donut Hole, but I rarely participated. "I mean, except for the luggage thing, and the broken leg. Besides that, things seem likable."

A big wind blew a branch of green leaves into the window of the waiting room. It was followed by a huge burst of rain.

"And the monsoon," I added.

"Monsoon? This is a normal day for us. Just wait. As sure as it gets dark, it'll be sunny in a few hours."

A nurse brought Shannon out in a hospital wheelchair. Finn took the chair from the nurse. "That's some cast," he said. "Let's go, shall we?"

8

We went to Ballymore in a very tiny car. It was so small, if we'd stood it up on its trunk, it could have been a soup can. I sat in the back with Shannon. We tried to stretch her leg over my lap, but that didn't work, so we extended it and the ginormous cast over the center console. It hit the dashboard. We might've been able to stick it out a window, but it couldn't get wet. Finn held her heel up so that it wouldn't bounce off the dash. The soup can driver, an elderly woman who didn't speak, drove much more slowly than the ambulance, but every turn made me jump because it felt like she was going the wrong way by driving on the wrong side of the narrow street.

"Hang on. We'll be at the castle in just a minute," Finn said.

"Castle?" I asked.

"Yeah. Castle Ballymore. That's where I live."

A *castle*? Dad had left out that little and very important detail. I was going to stay in a castle, like an Irish princess.

"Are you . . . um . . . I mean, you said you live there, so are you, or were you . . ." How could I ask this?

"She's trying to ask you if you're an orphan," Shannon finally explained.

"Oh. No, I'm not. Ballymore isn't an orphanage anymore, hasn't been for years. Now it's a bed-and-breakfast that my father runs. Besides my da, there are two men from the old orphanage who live there and help maintain the castle."

We drove down a bumpy road that wound through thick greenery. It had a going-to-the-Bat-Cave feel to it, and for a second I considered that they could be taking us to an actual cave. I might have been able to get away, because I'm a fast runner, but Shannon would have been a goner. Maybe I should've asked these people for some ID. With my luck recently, getting kidnapped seemed like the next natural step.

I checked out Finn's reflection in the side mirror. He wore a well-worn flannel shirt, the sleeves folded up above his wrists. There was nothing I saw that screamed, *Weirdo!*

I relaxed a bit and thought about the shower I couldn't wait to take at the castle. The bathroom at the castle was probably marble with multiple jets to spray hot water on me. The towels were probably plush and white. Oh, and I really hoped my private room would have a robe, slippers, and a huge canopy bed. I was dying to change into one of my travel outfits from Banana Republic and re-straighten my hair—then I remembered that all my clothes and my beloved flat iron were lost. But surely a castle would have a spare gown I could wear just for tonight, until my stuff arrived.

The rain lightened up, but the sky remained dreary. Shannon asked from the backseat, "So, Finn, what grade are you in?"

"I'm thirteen, but I'm not in a grade. I get tutored at the castle by the two live-in helpers. Oh, by the by, my da is fixing you a wonderful dinner tonight. He's a great cook."

"And what do you do for fun?" she asked.

"Well, my da and me, and the men from Ballymore, we help a lot around town. Like with the poor or the elderly. It can be pretty fun."

"That's so nice of you," Shannon said admiringly. "Not enough people volunteer anymore."

"We do, all the time."

I supposed that was good. But not exactly my idea of fun. Carissa probably would have said something that was borderline insulting, but I just didn't say anything. I had never met a real, live do-gooder before.

We approached a building that was obviously a castle, but not the Cinderella kind. It was the horror movie kind. All the vines were overgrown and crept up to the roof. Many of the stones in the walls were inched out of their original places, and moss stuck out between them, and the roof sagged in some places. Finn said, "Here she is. Castle Ballymore. Built in 980."

Nine hundred and eighty? *As in, over a thousand years ago?* I figured the stones had every right to inch out after holding up walls for more than a thousand years.

I said, "That was hundreds of years before Columbus even sailed the ocean blue and discovered America." The thought gave me goose bumps.

Standing to the side was a sign that read, CASTLE BALLYMORE. There was a sign next to it that had once said, HOME FOR BOYS, but some of those letters were gone.

The driver parked the car and took off very quickly into the barn. I called out a "Thank you," but I don't think she heard.

Finn and I realized pretty quickly that we weren't going to be able to get Shannon into the castle without a wheel-chair, which we didn't have.

Finn put two fingers together, put them into his mouth, and let out a screeching whistle into the rain. Two big men in sandals and overalls came out. Both held a biscuit in each hand.

"Hello!" they called. First one, then the other, enveloped me in a bear hug. They smelled like a combo of burlap and cinnamon sugar. With little talk they lifted Shannon, while still holding their biscuits, and brought her inside.

Finn closed the car doors. "That was Gene and Owen. They're my tutors. If you didn't notice the resemblance, they're brothers."

"Twins?" I asked.

"Actually, yes," Finn said.

"They do look a lot alike," I said.

"They act a lot alike too."

He gave me an *After you* gesture, and I proceeded toward the grand tall double doors, the wood patterned with knots. The doors were very heavy and creaked when I pushed them open.

If you imagine a castle as bright and sparkly with glass slippers, singing mice, and servants with white gloves, this was the opposite.

Gene and Owen had sat Shannon in a droopy armchair in front of a fireplace. A fire was already roaring, making the room cozy. They propped her foot up on a stool and rested a knitted blanket on her lap. In a moment she had a scone in her hand.

"Your luggage?" Owen asked.

Gene quickly explained that he'd already spoken to Dad, that the luggage was lost and the airport would call when they found it. "Can you take a peek in the community closet?" he asked Owen. To me he said, "We have lots of good stuff in there. Donations mostly. We share them with the needy, and I guess you're needy."

Owen retreated.

Donations? I didn't love the sound of that compared to a ball gown or my new jeggings. But I had nothing else, and I was touched by their willingness to share with a complete stranger.

A gray-haired man in jeans and an old T-shirt covered by an apron came out. He looked at me, and his eyes filled with tears. "Oh, my dear goodness," he said with a heavier accent than Finn had. "You look just like your da." He put his hands on my cheeks, and it was obvious that he'd been cutting onions.

"This is my father," Finn explained.

"I'm Den Leary. Call me Den or Leary, I don't care much. I'm just so happy that you're here." He removed his hands and sniffed back his emotions. "We're goin' to have a delicious feast tonight," he said. "Your da and I were boys here together. He left for America, and I stayed." When he said "I," it came out like "oy."

Den (or Leary) explained, "Your mum and Hope are napping, and Da is on his way here from the airport. He hasn't found your luggage, I'm sorry to say. The sister who talks a lot—"

"Piper," I offered.

"She is in the kitchen preparing a snack," he said. "The other sister. The one with the thick head on 'er—"

"Huh? Head?" I didn't understand.

"The one that's in a bad mood . . ."

"Eryn."

"I think she's gone for a walk in the rain." He added, "I thought that was strange."

"She does that," Shannon explained. "She isn't good

at regular human interaction. Don't take it personally."

"I see," Mr. Leary said. "For you McGlinchey girls, you can have anything you want. Just ask. It's no bother."

Shannon and I thanked him before he returned to the kitchen.

Then Owen came back with baskets of stuff for Shannon and me.

"I'll show you to your room," Finn said. "You can take a nap before an early dinner?" He said it like a question, with his Irish accent.

Rest sounded good. It had been a long day. Between the long flight and the traumatic, unexpected detour, I was exhausted.

"Meghan?" Finn asked me. I hadn't realized that I hadn't answered him.

"Yes." I snapped out of it. "A nap is exactly what I need." I looked at Shannon, who now had a mug of something hot in her hand. She didn't look tired at all.

Owen stoked the fire. "She can't go to her room without a snack," he said. "We don't nap on an empty stomach around here."

"I think I'm too tired to eat," I said. "Besides, I don't want to spoil my appetite for that feast."

"Oh-ho." Gene laughed. "That's right. Our dinners are wonderful. We eat well round here." He patted his belly. "In case you can't tell."

The flames lit up Shannon's face.

Owen and Gene each sat at her side, and the three of them talked and laughed like they'd known each other forever.

9

⚭

I followed Finn up a dark spiral staircase. About every third step had a pot or pan catching raindrops that seeped through the ceiling. The stained-glass windows lining the walls were streaked with rain.

This place was run-down for a bed-and-breakfast that people would pay to stay at. I wondered if they had other customers staying here this week. It was so quiet, I assumed they didn't.

Finn asked, "What are your plans while you're here?"

I didn't think it was a good idea to tell him his guest was cursed.

"We're going to meet with my dad's long-lost sister. At the Spring Fling."

"That'll be fun."

The hallway was very dark. Finn took a lighter out of his pocket and lit candle sconces on the wall as we approached a door. He pushed it open. It was black inside. Finn went ahead of me and pulled heavy drapes to the sides, letting in the only smidgen of light outside that wasn't blanketed by clouds. Then he lifted a big glass globe and lit an oil lamp. The whole thing felt *très* romantic.

The amber light of the lamp captured Finn's face like a close-up in a vampire movie, except his cheeks were rosy, not pale. He was actually cuter than I'd originally thought. Maybe he was cuter than the guys in my town, or maybe the fact that he was a mysterious foreigner in a candlelit castle made him more appealing.

"Meghan?" he asked. "What's wrong? You look like you've seen a ghost."

He'd caught me staring. *Ugh!*

He added, "Which is possible, because most of these old castles are haunted, and Castle Ballymore is no exception."

"Ghosts? No, I didn't see any ghosts. I'm just very tired, jet lag. But thanks for the tip. I'm sure the haunting info will help me sleep tonight." I put the basket of donated clothes down on the thin rag carpet. "I was just wondering if you had electricity. It's fine if you don't. I was just wondering."

"Nope. We don't have indoor plumbin', either. If you want to get an umbrella, I'll show you the outside toilet, or I can just bring you a bowl for . . . you know."

What!

I must've had a horrified expression on my face—an expression that I hoped wasn't rude—but I couldn't find a single word to respond.

After an awkward pause Finn said, "I'm kidding. But you should see your face." He laughed. Then he pointed to an outlet. "We have electricity. We try to keep our bills down because business hasn't exactly been booming."

"You don't say." *Who would want to stay in this place?* A castle sounded glamorous, but after a thousand years— blah!

"It seems everyone wants to stay in fancy hotels. But we do have a group of women staying with us now. You'll meet them at dinner. I'm sure the conversation will be very interesting."

"Why? What do they talk about?"

Finn smiled. "You'll see."

I looked around the room for the bathroom. "And the . . . toilet?"

"Down the hall and to the right. We have hot and cold water and we try to conserve. There's a tank in the shower. All you have to do is pull the string for the water. Help yourself," he said. "Oh, I know you said you weren't hungry, but I brought this in case you changed your mind." He set a banana on the nightstand, then moved toward the door. "If I can't get you anythin' else, Meghan McGlinchey, I'll see you at five o'clock for dinner?" Finn began to close the door, but he stopped before it shut the whole way. "Meghan," he said. "It's nice to have you, and your family, here."

He started to close the door again, when I said, "Finn." He stopped.

"What?"

"What's 'Finn' short for?"

"Finnegan. Finnegan Leary."

I nodded, and then he headed down the hall.

I sat on the single bed. No canopy, but there was a blanket. Another bed for Shannon sat on the other side of the room. The thought of Eryn and Piper sharing a room made me chuckle. The bed was very soft, droopy.

How many people over the last thousand years had slept in this room?

Had they been knights? Kings?

Probably none of them had sat thinking about Finn's blond hair and sparkling eyes.

I sifted through the basket of clothes. *Hmmmmm.* Nothing cute like my new clothes, that was for sure. And definitely no ball gowns. The clothes weren't even in my size. *Sigh.*

After an awesome power nap, I navigated the hardwood-floored hallway, guided by the sconce candles along the sides, to the shower. I paused and took the last few steps to the bathroom in the form of hops: two, one, two, one, one, two. I figured it couldn't hurt to do my hopscotch routine.

I stepped into the shower and pulled the string to the water tank the way Finn had explained. The water was superhot. The soap smelled like almonds and looked hand-carved.

I lathered all over, including my hair. It felt so good to finally shower. My stomach growled. I couldn't wait for the feast.

My hair wasn't exactly thick, but the curls were taking a while to de-sud. About halfway through rinsing, the water stopped.

I pulled the string. Nothing. I pulled again, harder. The tank was— What is the right way to explain this? It was EMPTY! But I wasn't done! There was still soap in my hair. What was I going to do? Staying soapy wasn't an option.

I wrapped in a towel and looked around the room for a water source. There was a pedestal sink. I tucked my head under it and turned the faucet on. The water was ice cold. My scalp was instantly numb, and I was cold all the way down to my toes. In a minute *that* water was gone too, leaving my head frozen but suds-free.

I shivered and growled, "Clare Gallagher." When I found her the next day, I might shake her hands right off. But first I had to survive a feast and a night in a haunted castle, and I wasn't going to hop the hopscotch pattern anymore. That clearly didn't work.

10

I smelled something unfamiliar as I approached the top of the castle's spiral steps. Looking out the window, I saw the rain stopping. The sun was setting, but it was light enough to see acres of farmland and a town, which didn't seem to limit its use of electricity. And, I guessed, it had plenty of hot water.

I shivered. The castle seemed damp, all the way through the rich red-papered walls and floorboards.

I found Shannon, her injured foot perched on an old-looking chair, sitting with the twin tutors. Her cheeks were flushed, and she laughed at their jokes.

I noticed something strange overhead. A beautiful ornate chandelier that hung at an uneven angle. It filled the room with a wonderful glow.

"'Ello!" Gene yelled. "Sit with us, Meghan."

"Look at you!" Shannon called. "All cleaned and changed." I'd braided my wet hair and put on a long dark skirt and long-sleeved button-up white shirt from the stuff provided in the community basket. I wasn't actually sure what the ensemble looked like, because I hadn't been able to find a mirror anywhere in the bathroom or bedroom. The outfit was clean and comfortable but far from fashionable.

Mom, Dad, and Hope came down the stairs. They were dressed in donations too—jeans and T-shirts. Hope wore footy pajamas. They must've gotten the normal basket.

The large wooden front door opened slowly, and in walked a drenched Eryn. "Why don't you hustle and change for dinner," Mom suggested.

Soon Finn appeared holding a platter. On it was a big piece of some sort of meat that still had hooves attached. I tried not to look at it. Behind him trailed Piper with a basket of steaming rolls. "I got the bread!" she announced. "*Hot* bread coming out! Here comes the *hot* bread!"

"Sit," Finn instructed me. He gestured toward a chair with a maroon velvet cushion, a dark wooden back as tall as me, and ornately carved arms. It was next to a roaring fireplace that was big enough to stand in. It took only a few seconds for me to completely thaw out.

Finally Mr. Leary joined us, sans the apron, and he rang a bell. At that moment Eryn reappeared in clothes that made my outfit seem cool: a denim jumper and a plaid shirt.

I tried to stifle my laugh.

"You have a comment?" she asked me, annoyed.

"Nope," I said, grinning.

She said, "Looks like someone accidentally bunked me with Piper, but I want to be with Meg. So I moved in there—not that I had much to move. Dad, what's the 411 on the luggage?"

"They said they'll call," Dad said. "That's all I know. They don't know where it is."

"Just grand." Eryn took a seat.

"About the roommate switch," I said shyly. "I was supposed to stay with Shannon."

"Wrong, butt—"

She trailed off as several women seemed to materialize out of the castle's cracks and crevices. One at a time they bowed slightly and sat in the chairs on either side of Eryn. They must've been the women Finn had referenced earlier.

Finn explained, "This is Mrs. Buck." Mrs. Buck stood

out because she was wearing a cape, not dissimilar to the cloak Frank-O wore during his show. But hers was black. I wondered if she'd gotten it from a donation basket. "She and her friends are on a silent retreat." I finally got the joke about interesting conversation.

"Why?" I asked.

"They believe it brings them inner peace. Every year at this time they pledge to be silent for ten days. They break their silence at the Spring Fling."

I nodded like it totally made sense, but what I was really thinking was, *HUH? Seriously?*

Piper said, "That's weird," and put the bread basket down. Then she put her hands firmly on her hips and said to Eryn, "I wanted to room with Meghan. You had no right to switch rooms without a family meeting. No right at all—"

"I'm in!" Eryn announced.

"What?" Dad asked, confused.

"I'm signing up for silent meditation." She looked at her watch. "Starting now."

"You can't do that," Piper said. "Mom, can she? Can she just decide she's joining a silent meditation without a family meeting? And—"

This time Mr. Leary interrupted her, as politely as he

could. "How about if we all sit down, whether we're silent or not. Dinner is getting cold."

Everyone did as he asked. I sat on one side of Finn; Mrs. Buck sat on his other side. I actually thought it was a great idea for Eryn to be silent. I might not be called any names for a few days, and I thought maybe Piper should join in too.

Finn passed the bread, and Owen filled the glasses with water.

While everyone was preoccupied with filling their plates, Finn lifted a Coke from under his chair and poured himself half. He looked at me and raised his eyebrows. I nodded, and he took my glass under the table and filled it.

How did he know I *loved* Coke? "Thanks." It wasn't cold, but it was still good.

Soon my plate was full (I pushed the mystery meat to the side), and lively chatter (except for Eryn and the silent ladies) began. While the ladies weren't speaking, there was a lot of charade-type communications, and giggles covered with hands or napkins.

It was a truly wonderful feast. I liked everything about it (except the meat) and everyone around the table (except for Eryn). And I liked the table, the castle, the fire, the candlelight.

"Guess what?" Shannon announced. "Owen and Gene have agreed to show me some historic landmarks."

"How are they going to get you around like that?" I asked.

"They've already thought of everything," she said.

This surprised me, because they looked like they thought of nothing more than food. They piled butter on rolls and stabbed their forks full of the meat and potatoes.

Shannon said, "Owen and Gene have a special car where I can keep my leg extended. I'm going to write an extra-credit paper for school!"

"Nerd," Eryn said.

"Silent," Dad reminded her.

She made an act of zipping her lips.

"Can I go?" Piper asked. "I like history. I like extra credit. I can write a paper too. Just like Shannon."

Finn eyed Tweedledee and Tweedledum at Shannon's mention of the vehicle. I caught the awkward gaze. "What? Is it a cow-drawn hay wagon?" I was totally kidding and expected them to laugh, but maybe they actually had cow-drawn hay wagons, because no one seemed to think it was funny.

"Not exactly," Finn said.

"It's a fine automobile," Owen said through a mouthful of food.

Gene repeated, "Fine automobile." He emptied his glass. "With plenty of room to lie down in the backseat!" He laughed with a snort.

Shannon narrowed her eyes at them. "What are you two up to?"

The large men were too busy laughing to hear her.

Finn said to Shannon, "It's our hearse. They're planning to take you in our hearse."

"What's a hearse?" Piper asked.

Gene shrugged. "It was a donation!"

My face froze. I wouldn't be caught dead riding around in the back of a hearse, but Shannon thought it sounded like fun.

"A few pillows, and I'll be traveling like a queen," she said.

Piper asked again, "What's a HEARSE?"

"A dead queen!" Gene yelled.

And we all laughed, even the ladies on their silent retreat. Then we all laughed at *them* because they were laughing, and soon my stomach was hurting and my eyes were watering.

"WHAT'S A HEARSE?" Piper asked, really loudly this time. Mom leaned in and whispered to Piper. "Ewwwww! I don't think I'll go with you."

I spread some white cream on my bread and bit into it. Maybe my face said, *Yuck*. This wasn't butter.

"It's goat cheese," Finn whispered. "Do you like it?"

It had taken me by surprise the first time, so I tried it again. Nope, still yuck. "Yes," I said.

Finn took the bread from me. "You're a bad liar," he said, and he ate it.

There was a lull in conversation, but only for a few beats before Piper took the opportunity to tell everyone, "Did you know Meghan is cursed?"

11

"Curse-hearse. . . . It rhymes!" Gene said.

The ladies giggled at his silliness.

"What's this about a curse?" Mr. Leary asked.

"Well, it's not a big deal, really," I said. "It's just a little dilemma caused by a chain letter."

Piper said, "Can you believe she *e-mailed* the three letters instead of regular stamp-and-envelope mailing them?"

There were gasps from the ladies, Owen, and Gene, who all, apparently, knew this was a no-no.

"I know, right?" Piper asked. "Who does that? I'll tell you who—Meghan McGlinchey. And as we know, that's cheating, so her bad luck began Friday—in a big way."

"I don't think they need to know the details," I said to

Piper. "She's making it sound much worse than it actually is."

"Are you kidding me? It was like a colossal fail." She stuck her arms out to the side like a cheerleader forming the letter F. "Listen to this. Her socks." She told them about my socks. I sank into my chair as everyone listened and laughed. "And her speech." Piper told the microphone story. More laughter. "If you think that was bad, listen to what happened at the magic show." As everyone listened to the horror story that was my life a few days ago, I slumped as low in the chair as I could get without going under the table.

Piper finished, "And *that* put her in the meanest teacher's office for the rest of the day, with enough demerits to give her a day's detention."

"It's under control," Shannon said reassuringly. "All Meghan has to do is find the other links of the letter and shake their hands. Then the curse will be lifted."

"How does that help?" Dad gave Hope a few peas, which she grabbed in her fist and smooshed into her mouth.

"They say that if I find the links and get them all to forgive me for e-mailing the letters, and double-shake on it, then the curse will be lifted," I explained. "It's the only way. I have to do it. Look at Shannon's leg. This can't keep happening, or I'll have to live all alone like a hermit."

"That's my girl," Dad said proudly. "Always with a plan."

Finn said, "So, you're pretty superstitious."

"I've always been," I said. "I remember my dad told me a story about a potato farmer who went out on Friday the thirteenth, joking about tales of the day's bad luck. He never made it to the pub and was never seen again. His wife died of a broken heart. Since they had no children, their land was given to the county and used as a dump."

"It's called Logan's dump," Mr. Leary added. He turned to my dad and added, "I think we heard that story here."

I said, "I've always been kind of weird about superstition and luck."

Finn slapped the table. "Then you need to find the links."

"You believe in chain letters?" I asked him.

Before Finn could answer, Owen said, "If you believe you're going to have bad luck, then you probably will."

"Amen," said Gene.

"I'm planning to talk to Aunt Clare tomorrow at the Spring Fling," I said. "She'll double hand-shake me, I'll find out who sent her the letter, and then I'll go find them." I had this all figured out. "Like you said, Dad, I'm a girl with a plan."

Dad's fork was halfway in his mouth when he pulled it out. "Aunt Clare? My sister's name is Colleen."

COLLEEN?

"And, I'm sorry to disappoint you," Owen said, "but the Spring Fling isn't tomorrow."

"Friday," Gene confirmed.

FRIDAY!

"I can't wait until Friday!" I cried.

Dad said, "Tomorrow Mr. Leary and I are going to visit old friends—guys who used to live here at Ballymore with us. We're spending the night up north. Then we have reservations for a wonderful boat ride on Tuesday. I'll take you to look for Clare on Wednesday. We can call your aunt Colleen and see if she knows her."

"Or I could take her," Finn said. "It will be an adventure."

"Excellent idea," Gene or Owen said—I wasn't sure which one.

I whispered to Finn, "Really? You would want to do this?"

Finn said, "Are you kidding me? Do you know how boring it is around here? If Shannon takes Owen and Gene, I'll have no one to talk to." He looked at the mute ladies, then at Piper. "I'm sure she's a very nice girl, but I don't know if I can handle a week of that."

I nodded. "I totally understand."

"Sound good, Da?" Finn asked.

Mr. Leary said, "It's not up to me." He looked at Mom and Dad and said, "I promise you that Finn is very responsible."

Owen said to Gene, "Finn's more mature than YOU!" He folded a hunk of meat in a slice of bread, added goat cheese, and wiggled it into his mouth.

Mom said, "That's a kind offer, Finn. But I don't think it's a good idea for the two of you to go around Ireland without an adult. Maybe Owen or Gene can take you and the other can go with Shannon to work on her extra-credit project?"

The twin tutors dropped their bread and looked at her like she had just suggested they visit the depths of Hades.

Finn clarified. "They like to be together, like a pair of socks."

Apparently they liked being compared to socks because they touched their glasses together and then clinked with everyone else, including me with my Coke.

Dad said, "I agree with your mom. I'm sure Finn is

responsible. Why don't you explore the town of Ballymore for two days. There's plenty of stuff to do right here. We'll do the boat ride, and then I'll take you out all day Wednesday. And in the meantime I'll call Colleen. Piper and Eryn can come too. We'll do some sightseeing."

"Dad, please, no," I said.

"Since Eryn's vow of silence, she hasn't called anyone names," he said, trying to convince me.

"OMG! Can I kiss the Blarney Stone? I love kissing rocks more than life itself," Piper exclaimed. "Although, I do wonder about the germs. Do you think they sanitize the boulder after each kiss? I hope so. If not, I'm gonna call it the Blah-ney Stone."

Dad said to me, "And I'll talk to her about her chattering."

It was settled. Dad would take me, Finn, Eryn, and Piper on Wednesday. Mom would stay behind with Hope. Shannon would hang with Owen and Gene. Until then we could walk into Ballymore Village and check things out.

It looked like things were finally looking up. Until my "luck" struck . . . *again.*

12

It started out small.

A crumb of plaster fell into my meat and spinach.

Then bigger crumbs of plaster fell onto Finn's and Mr. Leary's plates.

Mrs. Buck looked up, alarmed, and shouted, "Look out!" Before anyone could move, the crystal chandelier crashed onto the heavy antique wood table with a huge crash. Everything was crushed under its weight.

I think my heart literally stopped beating.

"Is everyone okay?" Mr. Leary asked.

Everyone nodded, except Gene, who wept.

"Are you hurt?" Mr. Leary asked him.

"No," he cried. "I'm still hungry."

"Well," Mr. Leary said. "That's why we have dessert. I'm just glad no one is hurt."

I wasn't close to *glad*. "It's the curse," I said. "I'm so sorry. I brought a curse into your castle. We have to leave. Dad, I am totally serious, we all have to leave now."

"I'm not exactly mobile," Shannon pointed out.

"Then we'll sleep outside or in the car. Or at least I will," I said.

Piper said, "I'm not leaving. Have you looked around? This is a castle, for Pete's sake! I'm not cursed. I don't see why I should have to leave if I don't want to."

"Wait just a minute," said Mr. Leary. "I have an idea. Why don't we ask everyone if they want you and your curse to sleep outside? If that's what they want, you go. If not, you stay. Okay?" He looked over the chandelier around the table at everyone to see nods and one raised hand from Owen.

Owen said, "I have a question. Would she go outside before or after dessert?"

"Does it matter?" Finn asked.

"Why, yes. I believe it does. What's for dessert?"

"Bread pudding."

"I daresay it matters quite a lot, then," Owen said. Gene nodded in agreement.

Mr. Leary said, "As soon as possible we would set Meghan up outside. Now everyone close your eyes."

I might *actually* be spending the night camping out in the rainy Irish countryside. Or worse, in the very small economy car with my legs all folded up. Or even worse still, lying out flat in the back of a hearse. They were all terrible options. I closed my eyes.

"Okay, everyone," Mr. Leary said. "Raise your hand if you're afraid of Meghan's curse and would prefer she slept outside."

Silence and darkness.

How bad will it be if I peek? I did it really superfast, and I saw Eryn's hand up, and others—one, two, three—before my eye closed. The other hands were from the ladies, who obviously wanted to complete their silent retreat without a chandelier crashing on their heads. They wanted me outside all alone!

"Okay, the majority has spoken," Mr. Leary said. "You may open your eyes."

I waited.

He said, "Meghan stays, and dessert will be served in the parlor. We'll take care of the mess later."

Gene looked up and mouthed "Thank you" in response to dessert.

Phew! I really didn't want to sleep outside. And I really, *really* couldn't wait until Wednesday to begin my search, which I suspected was going to take more than a day.

Owen and Gene helped Shannon to the parlor, and Mom excused herself to put Hope to bed. "Not without dessert," Mr. Leary said. "You can take a piece with you."

Mr. Leary retreated to the kitchen to get the bread pudding and new drinks for everyone.

On our way to the parlor, Finn said to me, "That was close. For a minute I thought I'd be bringing you a quilt under a willow tree."

I didn't smile. As mean as it was for those women to vote me out of the castle, they were the only ones other than me who were taking this full-scale curse seriously.

Finn followed me. "We'll have fun in Ballymore Village."

"I'm not sure I'm capable of having fun while I'm cursed. I would be too worried something bad would happen to someone. You shouldn't be around me."

He looked at Piper, who was retelling Owen and Gene the story about the magic show, then at Eryn, whose nose was glued to her phone. "I'm not going to be alone with the two of them in Castle Ballymore for two days."

Now, I don't think Finn realized how big a deal the next thing I said was. You see, I'm all about the rules. I follow them, and all is well. But I was cursed, so the regular rules didn't apply anymore. "I'm cursed, and I have to do something about it. Before Wednesday."

"What are you thinking?"

"Something that will get me in a heap of trouble," I said.

"Running away?"

I nodded.

"Not alone, you're not. You'll need someone to show you around," he said.

Before I could answer, someone behind us cleared her throat. I figured it was Eryn and the plan was a bust, but it was Mrs. Buck. She'd heard what I'd said, and she wanted us to know.

My heart thumped, and I looked at Finn with worry.

"Don't worry," he said. "She's cool. If she tells our secret, then I'll tell hers." She made an angry face when she heard this, and walked away.

"What's her secret?" I asked.

"C'mon. I'll show you real quick before dessert."

Finn led the way back through the dining room, across

the foyer, and into a very cold section of the castle. He stopped at a door that blended into the wall—a door that you could pass by easily—and slid it open, revealing a huge library. He lit a candle that gave just enough light for me to see shelves of books lining the walls.

"Let me guess. You and Mrs. Buck read together?"

His smile said it was more exciting than reading. Then, like in a spy movie, he pulled a book off the shelf, and it triggered a hidden door to crack open. Finn pushed it aside and gestured for me to go in.

"No, you first," I said.

I walked really close behind him with one hand on his back, so that I could tell where he was. Because it was so dark, I couldn't see until he tapped a switch. The room lit up, and I gasped. It was like we'd entered a different world. There were lights hanging from the ceiling over a pool table, a Ping-Pong table, and a foosball table. Arcade games were blinking and dinging along the walls. The machines played their theme songs loudly—an alien game, Ms. Pac-Man, and pinball, the old-fashioned kind like from the Donut Hole.

"What is this place?"

"The men who ran the orphanage stashed these

donations away. It was like a special secret place for the boys. Since it doesn't go with the atmosphere of the rest of the castle, we keep 'em hidden away. No one but me comes in here, except when Mrs. Buck visits. She's a closet gamer—these kinds of games, not the handheld ones. She sneaks down here, and we play all night sometimes.

"She doesn't really like the other ladies in her club very much," Finn continued. "So she came up with the idea of a silent retreat so she wouldn't have to talk to them. Then she sneaks down here and plays these old games that you can't find anymore. But she never breaks her vow."

"Ha! That is funny!"

"So, she won't tell anyone our plan. But she will be very bored without me."

Finn turned the lights off, and we returned to the parlor just as Mr. Leary was bringing out the bread pudding.

We all ate quietly. Slowly the ladies retreated back into their rooms. Mrs. Buck was the last to go, and before she did, she gave Finn and me a long stare.

Mr. Leary said, "You'll find gobs of history and lots to do in Ballymore Village. It isn't more than a stone's throw away. Finn knows all of the most interesting people there."

Piper said, "I love interesting people. And actually, they like me too because I'm interesting. Right, Dad?"

"Yes, you are, sweetie."

I smiled. "Here's to a great week for everyone."

13

The rest of the night was—how can I explain this?—awful! It was pitch black in my room. Every creak of the castle reminded me of curses and ghosts. The last time I'd woken up to look at the time on my phone, it had read two thirty. Finn and I had agreed that he would let me know when he thought the coast was clear.

"Are you ready?" I heard in my ear. I jumped. My first thought was that it was a ghost, but it was just Finn.

I said, "So ready."

"See you outside in five minutes."

The floorboards creaked as I padded down the stairs. I stopped because I thought the sound would wake someone up, then realized the whole place was creaking. The chandelier had been cleaned up (I assumed by Owen and Gene), and the massive table was set with new mismatched china for breakfast. I wondered what my parents would do in a few hours when they sat there and realized I was gone. One thing was certain. I'd be in *major* trouble. But I didn't change my mind. This was something I *had* to do, and if that meant I'd be punished—well, that was the price I was willing to pay.

I sat by the fire, where a few embers remained, and put on my sneakers. Then I pulled the heavy wooden front door open. Just a speck of sun rose over the horizon.

I'm really doing this, I thought.

Finn held the door to the soup can open and waved me in. Mrs. Buck was behind the wheel.

"What's she doing?" I asked him.

"It's perfect. She wanted to get out for a while, and now we also have an adult with us, so you can't get in trouble. She doesn't talk, so it'll be like she isn't even here," Finn said. "I call that a win-win."

I guessed it wasn't a completely bad idea. She seemed like a nice enough lady—a weird, silent, and caped lady, but nice enough.

"All right." I got into the backseat. Finn climbed in next to me.

"What are we telling our parents?"

"Mrs. Buck left a note that we're looking for links on the way to visit her brother for dinner. And she gave them her cell number."

I had to admit, it really did sound perfect. Then Finn asked, "So, what's the plan?"

"I'm going to call my newly found aunt Colleen and ask her if she knows Clare. I mean, they have the same last name. How else would Clare have gotten my address?" I fiddled with my phone. "The letter was postmarked from Limerick. There are fifteen Colleen Gallaghers there. I'll start calling them, I guess." I let out an excited laugh.

"Wait a sec," Finn said. "It's not even seven o'clock in the morning."

"Fine. I'll wait till eight."

"Umm, maybe nine."

"Eight thirty," I compromised.

Mrs. Buck drove down the bending road and passed Ballymore Village, which was as quaint as they'd said it was. If I hadn't been cursed, it would've been a cool place to spend a few days.

"Do you know how to get to Limerick?" I asked Mrs. Buck.

She gave me a thumbs-up.

The arch of the sun showed bright green fields, broken up by low rock walls that acted like fences. Some squared sections of the fields were a deeper, richer green than others. The pattern of oddly shaped squares continued over the low hills and as far as I could see.

At the sight of the sun, Mrs. Buck pulled goggles over her head and slipped on black leather driving gloves and gigantic headphones. From the nod of her head, it seemed that she liked what she heard.

We drove through Cork City and saw its colorful four-story row homes. "Why are these houses painted different colors?" I asked.

"The story goes that it's for men when they come home after a night at the pubs. The colors help them know which house is theirs."

"You're making that up," I said.

"I'm not," he said. "Apparently, after stumbling into the wrong home several times, someone had the idea to paint theirs a distinguishing color to make it easier to find. I don't know if it's true, but that's what I heard. And it makes sense."

As we left the city, we drove by pastures, each a darker and more brilliant green than the last. Sitting in some of the fields were chunks of crumbling stone wall that looked Gothic and ancient.

"What's that?" I asked, pointing at the rocky rubble.

Finn said, "This entire city was once surrounded by a tall stone wall. The people of Cork didn't venture out, and outsiders weren't allowed in."

"Why?"

"There were medieval battles for land and power. Vikings came from Scandinavia and would ruthlessly smite entire villages."

Smite? Not a Delaware word. *Oh, I love Finn's accent.*

He continued, "People who ventured to marry outside the walls were banished."

"Being banished is a little extreme, isn't it?"

"I don't know. They must've been very afraid of whatever was going on out there. I'm thinking dragons," he said. I didn't think he was serious, but I wasn't sure.

Driving in Ireland felt bizarre to me. Mrs. Buck drove

on the opposite side of the road. Little cars whizzed by us, fast, like there weren't any speed limits. If there were, they weren't really laws. They were more like suggestions.

Suddenly I remembered Carissa. I hadn't texted her since the hospital. I typed a very quick text: "The mission has started. All ok."

14

Sometimes, out of nowhere, a random sheep would just walk out into the road. As we kept driving, I figured with my current bad luck it was only a matter of time before we hit a sheep or a shepherd, or a car, or a building; or—

"What's wrong?" Finn asked.

I cracked the window open and took in a breath of fresh air. "I think riding on the wrong side of the road is making me a little carsick," I said, and put a hand over my stomach.

"Ever think *you're* the ones who drive on the wrong side of the road?" he shot back. "Do you want Mrs. B. to pull over?"

"No, I'm fine." But I wasn't fine; I was panicking a little. I mean, what if something cursed and terrible happened out here on the road? I reached into my pocket and palmed my rabbit's foot, which wasn't my favorite good luck charm, because I couldn't get over the fact that it had been very unlucky for the rabbit.

I sucked in the cool morning air until exactly eight thirty, when I dialed the first number for Aunt Colleen. It was wrong, but the woman was nice and told me who to call next. She was also the wrong one. I continued calling. Mostly they didn't answer the phone. Finn kept telling me it was because they were still asleep. I left messages on answering machines.

"I'll call them again in an hour." But we arrived in Limerick before that.

"The first thing we're gonna do is get us a burger," Finn said.

"It's early for a burger."

"Well, we have to eat something," he pointed out. "And we can try a local custom for finding someone."

"What?"

"We ask around and see if anyone knows them. It's low-tech, but it works more often than you would think."

"Ha-ha," I said. I got what he was saying, but I had my doubts.

Limerick bustled in the mid-morning. Both sides of

the cobblestone street were lined with two-story shops and restaurants with wooden tables and chairs set up outside. "Let's go in here." He pointed to a busy place called Kelleher's.

We sat at a mahogany table that had enough nicks and dents to be an English muffin. I wondered for a sec if the Irish called them English muffins or something else. Mrs. Buck made a funny movement with her thumbs and disappeared to a pinball machine in the corner. She kept on her goggles, headphones, and cape.

We ordered Cokes. They arrived in tall, slender glasses. The Coke was warm. "Finn?" I asked. "Do you think I could have some ice?"

He called to the waitress. "Some ice for the American, please."

She frowned but brought a glass of ice and asked me a hundred questions. What was my name? Where was I from? Was I related to Liam McGlinchey? Who'd made my scarf? Where were we staying?

Finn said to her, "We're looking for Clare Gallagher. Do you know her?"

To my surprise the waitress nodded. "Sure I do. Which one?"

15

⚬

"There's one-armed Clare; she lives on Post Street. And old Clare, who is in the nursing facility around the bend. Clare the baker. Clare the maid; she's nuts. And young Clare." She looked at the clock. "Young Clare should be here any minute for the Commencement."

"I think we're probably looking for young Clare," I said. "Although, I suppose she could have one arm. How old is that one?"

"About your age, I guess. They should both be here soon." She put a bowl of nuts on our table, and Finn ordered a sandwich. I got another Coke.

Finn said, "I guess we'll meet two of the Clares soon.

My money is on young Clare, because how could one-armed Clare write the letter?"

"She could write it with her one good arm," I said.

"Fifty percent chance that she can't."

I sipped my Coke, which was so much better cold. "Finn, you've gotta try this."

He took the straw out of his glass, put it in mine, and sipped. He winced at first, then tilted his head. "Not too bad." He put his straw back into his own glass.

"What's the Commencement?" I asked.

"It's the official start of the sheep hunt."

I was still confused.

He explained, "Every year right before the Spring Fling one sheep is marked with a big red bow around its neck. He wanders around the countryside. If you find him, and claim the ribbon, you get to be the guest host of the Spring Fling. It's an honor. The Commencement is when everyone starts looking for the lost sheep. It's also an excuse to have a street party. We do that a lot."

Within the next ten minutes the pub was packed. People of all ages, shapes, and sizes introduced themselves to me. These were really friendly people. I met a lot of girls named

Clare—all of them had two arms. None was referred to as "young Clare" and none of them had sent me a letter.

Soon there was a ruckus out in the street, and before I knew it, Finn was pulling me outside to the cobblestone sidewalk, into the thick of this Commencement.

Music started, people clapped, and I heard the sound of rhythmic clicking that I knew oh so well. I climbed up onto the base of a streetlight to see six girls Irish dancing—right there on the street. Their legs flew so fast, they were a blur. Their matching curls bounced as they slip-jigged from one side of the street to the other. I'm a really good Irish dancer, but these girls were great. Their ornate sequined dresses sparkled in the sun, making them look almost like magical . . . What are those forest fairies called? . . . Pixies! The dancing went on and on until in one perfect stomp they stopped.

Everyone cheered.

One man, an announcer of some kind who had a megaphone, went on to explain the rules for the sheep hunt, which Finn had already covered.

Then he introduced Kaitlyn, Sophie, Kiera, CiCi, Liadin, and Clare. Wait, could this be "young Clare"?

I inched my way through the crowd to get to her, and grabbed a sequined shoulder. "Clare?"

The girl turned around. "No, I'm Sophie. Clare is over there."

I found Kiera and Kaitlyn before young Clare.

Slightly breathless, I stood in front of her. "Clare?"

She nodded.

"I'm Meghan," I said. "I'm so glad I found you."

"Hello, Meghan. Thank you for watching the dance. Good luck with the sheep hunt." And she swung back into the crowd.

"Wait." But she was far away. "Clare! Wait!" She heard me and came back.

"Yes?"

"I'm Meghan. Meghan McGlinchey from Wilmington, Delaware. You sent me a chain letter?" I asked.

She stared at me like I was insane. "Meghan McGlinchey? Sorry. I've never heard of you."

16

I froze. "But you're Clare Gallagher, from Limerick, right?"

"Yeah, I am. But maybe you're looking for CiCi," she said.

"No. Thanks anyway, but I need to find Clare."

"CiCi *is* Clare. She's Clare Catherine. I'm Clare Rose. It gets confusing, so we call her CiCi. She's right over there."

I thanked her and ran in the direction she pointed. I found the curly-haired CiCi and tapped her gently on the shoulder. "Excuse me, CiCi?"

"Yes?"

"I'm Meghan McGlinchey, from Delaware."

"Oh!" she exclaimed. "My dear cousin! It's so good to finally meet you. I thought I had to wait until Friday, but here you are!" She gave me a huge hug.

"Cousin?" I paused. "Wait. Your mom's Aunt Colleen?"

"Yes. Of course."

I'd never had a cousin before.

She asked, "Did you get my letter?"

"I sure did."

"Wasn't it so cool—on paper and everything? I was very excited when I got an old-fashioned letter. I mean, who does that? I couldn't wait to send it to my friends. I just could not wait! Wasn't that so awesome to get it in the regular mail? And guess what?" She didn't wait for my answer. "Right after I sent you that letter, I won a big dancing trophy— really, really, really big! So I know the luck is real. It's real!" She hugged me again. "I am so glad it found you. What good luck did you get?"

My smile dropped, and I felt the excitement of my cousin discovery fade from my face.

"Oh, no. What happened?" she asked worriedly.

I explained it all, starting with the socks and ending with the chandelier.

"How could that happen?"

I closed my eyes so I didn't have to look at her when I said it. "I e-mailed it."

"What? Why did you do that? Why?"

"I wanted to be class president. I thought I could get good luck faster and win the election if I went the electronic route. Like, poof, instant luck! And now I'm cursed, and I have to find all the links to reverse the curse."

"Well, you and your boyfriend found me, so maybe your luck is starting to change." She referred to Finn, who stood nearby, listening.

"Oh, he's not my boyfriend," I said quickly.

Finn added, "Just friends. We just met."

"Really? Well, he looks like a nice friend, and I'm glad you're here. So glad. So glad!" She hugged me again. "Come on. Let's get a picture for our parents. They'll love it." She handed her phone to Finn. "Could you?"

One word kept repeating itself in my mind as Finn took our picture: COUSIN. I had a cousin. This was amazing. We were related through *blood*.

"Come on," she said. "Let me introduce you to all my friends." She looped one arm through mine and another through Finn's, like she was Dorothy and we were her Scarecrow and Tin Man, and dragged us toward the other dancers.

I asked, "Did one of them send you the letter?"

"Oh, no. That was Anna, another cousin. Anna O'Toole."

"Another cousin?" I asked. I'd thought I had none, and suddenly I had two! "How is that possible?"

"You know how cousins work. My mom and your dad are brother and sister. And his *other* sisters have kids, and they're your cousins too. And mine. They're your cousins and my cousins. We are all cousins!"

"I get that part. But, what other sisters? My dad thought your mom was the only one."

"No. There are two more. Three sisters altogether. And three is my luckiest of all numbers."

"Three! My dad is gonna go bananas. He doesn't know that!" CiCi squealed at all of this excitement. I couldn't wait for her to meet Piper. They were like two leaves on the shamrock.

"Please stay and hang out with me?" She squeezed our arms, through which she was still looped.

"That sounds like fun," Finn said.

"I think so, Finn," she said. "You know, I like that name."

I felt a drop on my arm. "Is that rain?" I asked.

"It always rains here." She held out her arms and did a little twirl in the drizzle.

Instantly my hair started to scrunch up. Ringlets pulled out of the braids like they wanted to remind everyone that

I was cursed and I couldn't hang out—I had to move ahead on my journey to the next link.

CiCi stopped twirling long enough to notice. "Yikes!"

"I know," I said. "This isn't good. I need to find Anna right away. My flat iron is in my lost luggage."

"Where does Anna live?" Finn asked.

CiCi shied away and batted her lashes a bit, like maybe she was flirting with him. "Rhymes with 'blue castle' and starts with an N."

"Newcastle?" he guessed.

"Ding! Ding! Ding! You win! Then she flipped her blond, bouncy curls off her shoulder in a way that could mean only one thing, no matter which side of the Atlantic you were on—she liked Finn.

I tried to distract her from him. "You know, I Irish dance too."

That got her attention. "It's in your blood, I guess. Maybe we can do a two-handed reel at the Spring Fling. Finn, will you be there too?"

"He will," I said. The rain picked up. "We have to go find Anna. It's very important we talk to her as soon as possible. Where in Newcastle does she live?"

"Oh, yay! You'll love her. But she's not home. She's at

the Newcastle tourney this week. Give her love for me." She hugged me again, then skipped in her hard-soled shoes into the crowd.

"Wait!" I called.

She turned. "What?"

"I need to shake your hands, assuming you'll forgive me for e-mailing the chain letter."

"Of course."

She double-shook like she did it all the time. Then Finn and I went to find the goggled, caped, headphoned, silent pinball player.

17

I was so psyched to find Anna, not only to reverse the curse but also to meet another cousin.

All kinds of thoughts were swirling around in my head after the excitement of the morning, the kind that make your brain feel like it's exploding. "Finn!"

He jumped. "What's wrong?"

"I've never had a cousin! I feel totally different knowing I'm part of a bigger family."

"What does it feel like?"

"I can't put my finger on it. It's a certain *je ne sais quoi*."

Finn added to my racing thoughts, "Not only do you *have* cousins, but you're *someone else's* cousin."

"Wow!" I said. "That's major! *Je ne sais What-What*."

I raised my palms to the roof of the tiny car.

Finn looked confused. "Must be an American thing."

I took my hair out of the braid and tousled the curls around. "And you know what else? My dad has three sisters! He is going to be shocked and so, so happy. I can't believe he doesn't know. *I* know and *he* doesn't know," I added.

"We have to go to Newcastle. Right now."

Mrs. Buck pulled out of our parking spot on the cobble-stone road. Then I kind of freaked a little more. "Wait! Listen to this amazing idea!"

"I'm listening," he said. "I like *amazing* ideas." He tried to imitate me but didn't do a great job.

"I'm not going to tell my dad about the other sisters."

"But you just said he'd be so happy."

"Oh, he will be when I *surprise him* with *all* of them— sisters, brothers-in-law, nieces, nephews—at the Spring Fling. Won't that be the biggest best surprise ever?"

"A great surprise."

"How long till we get to Newcastle?" I asked Mrs. Buck. She didn't hear me. So I lifted one of her headphones and asked again. She shrugged.

Finn guessed, "I think we'll get there before dinner. This little car doesn't go very fast."

"Dinner? I don't think I can wait that long."

"You'll make it," Finn said. "Let's make our plan, and that will distract you from the time."

"Fine. What's this tourney that CiCi mentioned?"

"It's a rugby tournament. That's huge around here. People travel all over to watch their favorite teams. It shouldn't be hard to find a big tournament in that small town."

For a second I thought about rugby, but soon my mind wandered to a scene I imagined in a snow globe: I unveil a bunch of long-lost relatives to my father at the Spring Fling. He cries in happiness. It's me, his middle daughter, who made it all possible. "Meghan," he says, "how can I ever thank you?" And I say, "You don't have to thank me, Dad. But there's a pair of UGGs I've been wanting, and maybe a Coach bag." And he says, "Anything. Whatever you want for the rest of your life, you can have." And that makes Eryn really mad and jealous, which makes me really happy.

I replayed the scene over and over in my head. I was going to be, like, the hero of the McGlinchey family, and probably the whole Spring Fling.

The car started slowing down for seemingly no reason.

I thought maybe Mrs. Buck was pulling over to look at a map or to show us something, but there was nothing to see other than a green pasture, tall grass, and blue sky. The car stuttered to a stop.

Something wasn't right.

"Why are we stopping here? What's going on?"

Finn leaned over the front seat and looked at the dusty control panel. "Ran out of petrol," Finn said with his palms up, as if to add, *C'est la vie.*

This wasn't *la vie.* This was *la curse.*

"Well, that doesn't sound good," I said.

"Actually, it's no big deal. These towns are far apart, and these little cars don't hold much, so it happens sometimes." He looked out the window at the sky. "We're lucky. It stopped raining." He pointed to a puff of white in the sky. "And see that?"

"The cloud?"

"It's smoke—from a fireplace. Someone's burning peat. There must be a house over that ridge. Let's walk over."

Finn and I walked through the tall wet grass toward the yucky-smelling smoke. Mrs. Buck stayed with the car.

In a small valley we found a thatched cottage that looked very much like the one from "Hansel and Gretel."

Wait. Hold on. In that story didn't some lady or witch try to shove the boy and girl into her oven? Or did I have that confused with another tragic fairy tale?

I didn't think that going to that house with a curse hanging over my head was a good idea.

18

I looked back at the field we'd walked through. We'd left no bread crumbs. What if we just disappeared?

Would Mrs. Buck come looking for us?

Would she break her silence in order to tell the police about two missing teens?

"Finn, maybe this isn't a good idea," I said.

"Why?"

"Well, they're, you know, strangers."

"If you don't talk to strangers, how will you ever make any new friends?" He gently knocked on the door. "How much are you willing to bet they offer us food?" he whispered.

Before I could explain to him about how we could be

locked in an oven, the door opened. A woman with a paisley handkerchief tied around her head answered. "What perfect timin'. I was just finishin' da soda bread. Come in." We went in. The door shut behind us with a loud click of the latch. The house might have looked like a sweet little cottage, and smelled like baking bread, but it felt like bad luck.

"What can I do for you?" She poked at the fireplace with a rod that reddened at the end.

Finn and I sat down. "Our car ran out of petrol on the other side of the field. We're hoping you can help us," Finn said.

"You're not the first traveler to come here with an automobile problem. Be a dear and help me here?" she asked me. I followed her into a very small kitchen. She handed me two pot holders. "I'll open the oven, and you take the loaf out, eh?"

"Out of the oven?"

"Tat's right."

This is what I figured was going to happen: I would lean in to get some loaf that supposedly was in the hot oven, and she'd shove me in, close the door, and bake me for dinner.

Would Finn try to save me?

I looked back at him—totally relaxed.

Maybe he was in on it?

It was kind of convenient that we'd run out of gas right by this cottage, wasn't it? I hadn't even checked to see if the gas gauge was really on *E*.

She asked, "Can you do that?"

"All right," I replied, because that was the way I was—a helpful rule follower. (Except for running away from the castle, which hardly felt like running away anymore because we had an adult and we'd left a note with our phone number. But we had taken off under the cloak of darkness, and at least that had *felt* against the rules.)

She opened the oven, and I took out the loaf, lightning fast, and put it on the counter. I dropped the pot holders and ran back to Finn. "Yer a quick one," the woman commented. She closed the oven and moved the loaf of bread onto the table. It smelled so good. Maybe I'd misjudged all of this. But then the woman held up a big, fat, shiny knife.

"Watch out!" I yelped at the sight of the blade.

"What's that, dear?" she asked, cutting into the bread. "Do you need the toilet?"

"Oh," I said, trying to calm myself. "Uh, no. Thank you."

She turned her back to us and opened an old-fashioned-looking fridge.

Finn looked at me, concerned, and mouthed to me, "You okay?"

I nodded and exhaled.

The lady returned with a small glass bowl filled with creamy, white butter.

"What are your names?"

"I'm Finn from Castle Ballymore. And this is Meghan."

"People call me Honey. I'll go to the barn and check for the petrol. You make yourselves cozy."

Finn buttered his bread. "I love soda bread."

"I've never had it."

"What kind of Irish American are you?"

"The kind whose mom works a lot and who doesn't have a grandmother." I looked at the bread. "Are you going to eat that? We don't even know her. How do you know it's safe?"

"I'll take a bite, and if I die instantly, then it's not safe, and you shouldn't eat it." He bit. Swallowed. A second later he grabbed his throat and started gagging.

Poison!

Finn made a gurgling noise from his throat that didn't sound exactly like choking, but then again, I'd never seen anyone being poisoned before. I was standing over him, ready to do CPR, when I noticed that he wasn't choking;

he was laughing. He wiped tears from his eyes and tossed another chunk of bread into his mouth.

"Not funny," I said angrily.

"It was a little funny. You should see your face."

I figured everything was safe, so I tried a piece of the bread. It was kind of like a cross between cake and bread, with raisins. And the rich whipped butter melted right into it. "I always wanted a grandmother." I looked at the soda bread and the cottage. It all felt very grandmotherly, once you got past the "Hansel and Gretel" thing.

"Are your grandparents alive?" Finn asked.

"My mom's parents died before I was born. You and your dad probably know more about my dad's family than I do."

Finn shook his head. "All I know is that your father's father died young and something happened to separate the rest of the family. Your father came to live at Ballymore Home for Boys, which is where he met my da when they were about six. A few years later a nice couple—your grandparents—took him to America."

"Why America?" I asked.

"I guess because there were more opportunities there," Finn said.

Honey came back into the cottage. "Sorry. I've some

bad news. No petrol." She held up an empty can. "I got bicycles in the barn. You're welcome t' borrow dem."

I thought we'd follow her outside to get the bikes. Instead she sat down and slathered a piece of bread. She *"Mmmed"* as she savored the bite.

She asked all about Ballymore, the weather, and the current rankings of the rugby teams. I was anxious to leave, find Anna, plan the huge surprise for my father, and undo a curse, but Honey was very interested in visiting with us.

Before we left on the bikes, she gave me a paisley handkerchief like hers, which I tied around my bulging curls. I was turning to wave good-bye, when I saw something I hadn't noticed on the way in. It was a rock with one word etched on the side.

O'Toole.

19

∂ℓ∂

"That's Anna's last name!" I went back to the door. "Are you an O'Toole?"

"You mean the rock? No, that was here long before I moved in, but it's too heavy to move."

I slumped onto the bike. For a second I'd thought I'd gotten lucky.

And guess what happened then? It started to drizzle. Again.

"What's with the weather here?" I asked Finn.

"It's an island. We get a lot of rain. But just look around at what we get for it, all of this beautiful green." We called Mrs. Buck and told her we would pedal to Newcastle, look for Anna, get gas, and bring it to her. She really couldn't argue. My back and legs got plenty wet on the ride.

"It's only about fifteen miles," Finn called over his shoulder.

Only fifteen miles? Pedaling was really hard, and Finn was getting far ahead.

I looked down and noticed that my back tire wasn't exactly round. It was more like egg-shaped, which made it turn with a little hump each time around.

Snow globe moment: I'm riding a broken bike through Ireland in the rain wearing donated clothes, and a handkerchief on my head, with a boy (correction—a cute boy) who I've known for about twenty-four hours. If you look closely, you can see that the girl in the glass globe is developing blisters on her bottom. She wipes rain off her face, and she feels the beginning of a *très grand* zit.

After what seemed like forever, we finally leaned our bikes against some trees near the center of town. The streets were much quieter than in Limerick. A few people lingered at shop windows, and some rode by on bikes with baskets of groceries.

I was wet but not soaked. Just enough to look like a sponge but not a mop.

A kid sat on a bench fiddling with his cell phone, with

a hypnotized look on his face. He wore a long-sleeved shirt with a collar and a team logo that I recognized as a rugby team's. He was probably in the tournament.

Finn said, "Hey, guy, did you play today?"

"Yup." He pushed buttons on his phone, hard, and tilted the screen to the right and left.

"Where is everyone?"

"Gone home. Tourney's been over for hours." He let out a frustrated groan and finally raised his head, totally annoyed with us for interrupting his game. "It'll start again in the morning, around seven." He went back to his game, clearly not interested in making friends.

I slumped. "Tomorrow?" Why should I have been surprised? Of course Anna wasn't here. I was cursed. I should've expected it.

"At least we know where she'll probably be tomorrow," Finn said. "Let's get some gas." At this point I was wet, tired, sore, and hungry. "Then we can get ourselves back to Ballymore."

"We're so close *now*. If we leave, what if we can't come back tomorrow? Plus, I know those ladies on silent retreat don't want me there."

"You peeked at the vote?"

"Just for a sec—long enough to see their hands up."

"In their defense, a five-hundred-pound chandelier had almost just killed them."

"Didn't Mrs. Buck say we were going to her brother's for dinner? Can't we stay there?"

"I guess we can ask her when we get back to the car."

The clouds finally moved aside to let the day's last rays of sunshine warm our backs. That was when I saw it on the side of the lane. It was purple and puffy and growing from a crack in the sidewalk. "Look at this, Finn." I bent next to the flower. "It's pretty."

"It's more than pretty. It's a thistle. And that's the sign of good luck. We should go this way." Then from right up ahead of us came a speedy tractor, the soup can right behind it.

Honey was behind the wheel of the tractor. "Got you two some petrol."

It was truly good luck for the blisters on my butt. Honey helped us get our car, which was driven by our goggled lady, and extra gas. We gave her the bikes. And, perhaps best of all, she invited me into the tractor to give me another loaf of soda bread.

While I was thanking Honey, Finn somehow communicated with Mrs. Buck. He told me, "Her brother is expecting us. She already texted with your parents and my da, so we can spend the night there."

"That's great news!" I hugged him. Then I went back to the crack in the sidewalk and picked the thistle. I was going to keep that puppy close to me.

We were climbing into the back of the soup can when I asked, "Do you think we can stop at the store so I can get a few necessities?"

"Like what?"

"Pajamas, toothbrush, shampoo. You know? Necessities." I left out clothes, shoes, mousse, hair dryer, flat iron, lip gloss, and skin cream.

Mrs. Buck navigated a roundabout—a circular island in the middle of the road that you need to go all the way around in order to turn—and pulled up at a small convenience store that looked like a 7-Eleven.

"How about a mall?" I asked.

"Mall? Is something wrong with this?" Finn asked. "This place has all the stuff you just mentioned."

I sighed. How could I buy clothes at a place like this? I mentally willed my luggage to find me while I squeezed the thistle stem.

We went into the store and I quickly filled a cart with

undies, toiletries, and makeup. I couldn't find a single item of clothing I'd wear. I got a T-shirt to sleep in. Then I grabbed a duffel bag, crackers, candy bars, and a few cans of Coke, too.

Finn looked at my cart in amazement. "That's a lot of necessities." He lifted a pink razor and quickly dropped it like he'd just touched a snake.

"Do you need anything?" I asked.

He held up a toothbrush. "This'll do it."

Mrs. Buck held one up too and smiled.

At the last second I picked up two postcards of Newcastle. One for me and one to send to Carissa, who had never responded to my last text. Weird. I paid with my emergency credit card. This was, after all, an emergency.

We drove for only a few minutes before Mrs. Buck parked. We followed her down a cobblestone sidewalk. Streetlights had come on, and the night was very clear. The smell of peat still lingered in the air. I was getting used to it, but I didn't like it. It was like smoking dirt or mulch mixed with a litter box—not like wood at all. One by one the stars popped out.

Finn looked at them. "I love the stars," he said.

I looked. "Me too."

"I think it's cool how wherever you are you have the same stars."

"Yup." I looked at the stars again. It *was* a cool idea, and something I never would've thought about.

We stopped at a small house with candles lit in each window.

"Looks like we're here," Finn said.

20

❧

We could hear loud Irish music through the front door of the row home. The high-pitched sound of a flute and the fast strum of a banjo instantly made me tap my foot.

Mrs. Buck knocked on the front door, and after a minute when no one came, she knocked more loudly.

There were several seconds of pots banging and clanging or furniture falling before the door opened and revealed a leprechaun. Well, at least this guy looked just like something between a leprechaun and a man.

"Aha!" the leprechaun said, and he hugged Mrs. Buck and picked her up. "Come in. Come in." His face was red, his hair light blond.

The house smelled like he'd been baking cookies.

The music was louder inside than it had been on the front stoop. He raised his elbows and kicked his heels as he made his way to an old record player and turned down the volume. It gave me a quick sec to look around the house.

Every surface was covered with doilies and knickknacks: cats, teacups, fancy glass bottles. . . . The overcrowding of stuff and the smell of Christmas gave the place a very homey feel.

"Welcome. I'm Paddy Flanigan. I love having guests!"

I couldn't imagine being excited to have strangers spending the night. Our house was all chaos all the time. Never baking. The only music was Piper singing. No one wanted to hear that, trust me.

"How ya been, Sis?" Paddy asked Mrs. Buck.

She gave him a thumbs-up. He did the same, laughed with a snort, and asked, "What's this all about?"

Finn explained that Mrs. Buck was in silent retreat. Paddy asked in a very loud and slow voice as though his sister was deaf, "TEN DAYS?" He held up all ten fingers.

"She can hear just fine," Finn clarified.

"Oh, how silly of me. Of course she can. OF COURSE YOU CAN!" he said to Mrs. Buck. "Really, TEN DAYS?

Actually, don't answer that if you can't talk. . . . YOU CAN'T TALK," he repeated.

Mrs. Buck nodded.

"Oh, you're right," Paddy said. "I think she hears just fine.

"Follow me now," he continued, and scurried down a slender hallway doing a quickstep. "Here we are. The lily room. Just right for spring, don't ya think? My sis and the lass can sleep here, and the lad can use the sofa."

We thanked him.

He said, "My third wife, Elizabeth, God rest her soul, she got laryngitis once and lost her voice for three days. . . .

"A cup of tea will crown ye. Out back," he said, and dashed away.

I asked, "What did he say?" I dropped my duffel.

"He's bringing tea to the backyard for us."

Mrs. Buck directed us to the back door, while she headed toward the kitchen. Finn went outside first, and he had to bend down so that his head wouldn't hit the top of the doorframe. I walked through with no problem.

It was a postage-stamp-size backyard surrounded by a fence that crawled with ivy. A wrought iron table and two chairs sat in the grass.

Paddy darted out through the low door. In a flash the

table was covered with cookies, cheese and crackers, and tea. It was just what I needed, because I was famished, despite the big piece of soda bread I had eaten earlier.

Paddy asked, "A bit of cow in your tea, lass?"

"Huh?"

Finn interpreted, "Do you want milk in your tea?"

"Oh, yes please."

"Gimme a ring if you need me." Paddy left a golden bell on the table.

I nibbled on a cookie. "I can feel my luck changing since we found CiCi and have gotten closer to Anna. Can't you?"

He leaned close to me and lifted the four-leaf clover off my neck. "You really believe in luck, don't you?" He dropped the silver chain and sat back with a cookie.

Then I toyed with the clover. "Do you think I'm too superstitious?"

"I don't know. Maybe you're just the right amount and I'm not enough."

"Don't you have any good luck charms? Something that when you see it or hear it, or whatever, it makes you think it might be lucky?"

"Well, I guess I have a favorite number. Maybe I think it's lucky."

"You do? So do I. What's yours? Wait. Let me guess. Four?"

"No."

"Nine?"

"No."

"Odd or even?"

"Even."

"Mine too. Maybe it's the same. Is it ten?"

"No. Yours is ten?"

"Yup," I said.

"Well, that's kind of cool." He held up his wrist. "Look at the time. It's twelve minutes after ten. Your lucky number is ten and mine is twelve, so between the two of us, this is a very lucky minute." We looked at his watch, which changed to thirteen after ten. "And it's over."

I said, "Now I'm always going to think of you when it's 10:12."

He spread some cheese on a cracker. "I like that. Kind of like a secret code."

"Kind of." We munched quietly.

"I've been wanting to ask you something," Finn said.

"Sure. What?"

"It's about your cell phone. Do you have games on it, like that guy on the park bench?"

"Oh, yeah. That phone has everything. You can totally use it. But—"

"What? If you don't want me to use it, I understand."

"No. It's not that. It's just that I don't remember seeing it lately. I'll be right back."

I hustled to the lily room and scrambled through my purse and new duffel full of stuff. Shoot! My phone wasn't there. How could I possibly live without my phone?

I gave Finn the bad news and held back my tears. He assured me that it would be okay. "I don't have one, and I get along just fine."

"But I'm used to texting and looking things up online and stuff."

"You'll survive. Those ladies don't talk for ten days, and they manage."

"Could you live without your games for ten days?"

"Well, you got me there. Probably not. It's only been one day, and I feel a little itchy." Then he said, "You know, you could help me with that."

"You want me to scratch your back?"

"No. You can play a game with me."

"I don't have a phone. What are we gonna play? Tag? Red light, green light? Hide-and-seek?"

He got up and went inside. "Fine," I said. "I'll count to twenty, and then I'm coming to find you." I started counting, and I felt ridiculous, like a ten-year-old. ". . . Nineteen! Twenty! Ready or not—"

He came back outside, ducking as he passed through the door. "What? 'Ready or not' what?" He sat again and put boxes on the table: dominoes, Scrabble, and checkers.

"Umm, I was going to say— Never mind. You seriously want to play a board game?"

"We don't have a pinball machine anywhere nearby. And I love these games. Which one do you want to start with?"

"Checkers, I guess. You might have to remind me how to play."

Finn looked at me like I was crazy. "You don't know checkers?"

"I do. I just kinda forgot. But I'll remember when you tell me."

We played until Paddy came out in his green, one-piece footy pajamas and told us it was past midnight.

I went into the lily room and took the empty twin bed. I fell asleep to the sound of Mrs. Buck's snoring.

21

I woke to the smell of bacon frying.

Mrs. Buck was nowhere to be found. I quietly walked down the hall in my socks and saw Finn on his stomach on the small couch. His feet extended over the armrest.

I left him sleeping and went into the kitchen, where I heard voices—as in *two*. Mrs. Buck flipped a deck of cards in a game of solitaire. Paddy started singing.

"Who were you talking to just now?" I asked Paddy.

"Talking? Don't be silly. Just me singing." He flipped bacon. "You slept well, did ye?"

"Yes, sir. Very well. Thank you." They didn't fool me. Mrs. Buck had been talking to Paddy. I'd just caught her cheating on her silent retreat.

Paddy poured me orange juice. It was thick and pulpy. (I like it thin and watery.) "I'm preparing you a full Irish breakfast," he said. "I hope you're hungry." Something sizzled. "Where's your friend? Still sleeping? Go and fetch 'im, or his eggs'll get cold."

Finn appeared before I could get up, rubbing his eyes.

Paddy said, "There you are, sleepy one. Sit yourself down." He spooned an undercooked sunny-side-up egg onto each of our plates. (I like them scrambled and well done.) Then he opened the oven, stepped up on a little stool, and took out a cookie sheet of biscuits. He gave us each two. From another frying pan he lifted two slices of browned tomato each, and finally he served several thick pieces of very fatty bacon. The whole breakfast looked undercooked and—what's the right word?—soggy.

Finn and Mrs. Buck dug in.

I ate the biscuit. I broke the egg yolk and swished some stuff around on my plate to make it look like I'd eaten the rest. Finn saw what I was doing and took one of my slabs of bacon. Paddy caught him.

"Somethin' wrong, m'dear?" Paddy asked me.

"No, no," I said. "It's a lot, and I'm not very hungry."

"You need to fatten your little self up. A bird never flew on one wing, you know. I'll make y'another egg," Paddy Flanigan said. Before I could protest, I heard an egg drop into the hot pan.

Suddenly Paddy screeched. At first I thought he'd seen Finn snatch another piece of bacon off my plate and he was offended. But then he yelled again, too forcefully for it to be about bacon. Finn jumped up to help him. The sleeve of his shirt flamed at the stove's burner.

Finn kicked the stool over to the sink and pushed Paddy onto the stool so he could reach the water that Mrs. Buck already had running. Tears ran down Paddy's face. "Oh, dear. Oh my. Am I scarred for life?"

Finn looked at Paddy's wrist. "It's a little red, but that's all."

His words calmed Paddy. "Thank you, lad." He sniffed back a tear. "I'm going to dress it. You help yourselves to more juice." He shuffled down the hallway.

Finn said, "That was close."

"Too close," I said. "You know what that was all about as well as I do. We have to hurry and find Anna O'Toole right away. Can we go? Now? Like *right* now?"

Finn didn't protest but shoved another piece of bacon into his mouth and wrapped a biscuit in a napkin. "I'm ready."

Mrs. Buck pointed to herself and held up two fingers. *Me too.* She put the playing cards into her pants pocket.

22

We drove away in the soup can. Mrs. Buck tapped the horn, and we all waved to Paddy. Then Mrs. Buck took out the goggles and big headphones, put them on, and moved her lips to the song on the radio.

"What if Paddy Flanigan had gotten seriously hurt?" I asked Finn as we sat smooshed in the back of the soup can. "What if his house burned down all because he was making an egg for me?"

"But none of that happened. He had an accident. His shirtsleeve was too long. And we were there to help. That's a good thing."

Did he seriously believe that or was he just trying to make me feel better?

"I wouldn't be able to forgive myself if my curse hurt you."

"That's okay, because you're not goin' to hurt me, and if you did, by accident, I'd get over it," he said. "I might not let you play my Alien Attack arcade game for a little while, but I'd get over it eventually."

I smiled, but I was still worried.

"Why don't you look out the window for the lost sheep," he suggested. "It'll keep your mind off the chain letter."

The fields to either side of me were filled with white wool. "There are a ton of them. Finding one with a red ribbon is probably impossible."

"That's why it's an honor. If it was easy, just anyone could win."

I pointed to a group of sheep. "Why do those sheep have blue paint on their fur?"

"It's wool, not fur," he said. "Farmers let their sheep wander all around the countryside, so they mark which ones are theirs with a color or a brand."

"What if the farmer who is blue decides to go out one day and paint a few thousand extra sheep blue?"

"You mean like to nick them?" Finn thought. "No one has ever actually done that, as far as I know."

"Finn, can I ask you a personal question?"

"Sure. Shoot."

"If you live and get tutored at the castle, where do you make friends?"

"I do a lot of volunteering with some other guys my age."

That didn't get me exactly what I was looking for. "What about *other* friends?"

"Like who?"

I think I blushed.

"Are you asking me about girls? Like, do I have a girlfriend?"

I shrugged and lowered my voice, although I was pretty sure Mrs. Buck couldn't hear a thing with those gigantic headphones. "I was just curious." I didn't want him to think I was interested for me, but maybe for a friend. Like, CiCi would probably ask me, and what would I tell her?

"I know some girls. I like them, as friends, but none as a girlfriend. I mean, I *like* girls, just not one certain special girl right now," he said.

I moved my face toward the open window. The car was silent.

Suddenly the road disappeared into a field of white. Hundreds of sheep were crossing the street in front of us. Mrs. Buck slowed down as they surrounded us. She honked and inched the car forward, but they didn't move. She honked again. Nothing. These were stubborn sheep.

Mrs. Buck put the car in park. Finn rolled down his window and let the warm sun shine on his face. The smell of burning peat filled the car. I was getting used to it now. I reached into my purse for my phone, but remembered it wasn't there. *Bummer!*

"We could be here awhile," he said. "Why don't you tell me stuff about you now."

"Me? Okay. I study hard to get good grades so I can get into a good college. I want to be a doctor, I think. I practice my Irish dancing for twenty minutes each night—"

Finn interrupted, "Why twenty?"

"That's my lucky number times two."

"Of course."

"I go to church on Sundays, eat five servings of fruits and vegetables each day—"

"Why five?"

"That's what's recommended."

"Uh-huh."

"I floss every day, go to sleep by ten o'clock."

"Why ten?" he asked.

"That's my bedtime."

"Gotcha."

"And I guess I just try to be a good person," I added.

"What about fun?"

I said, "I have fun."

"If you say so," he said, and smirked.

"Really, I do. My bestie, Carissa, and I go to the movies, bake cookies, go ice-skating, and one time we went indoor go-karting. It turns out that I'm an amazing race car driver. If I don't become a doctor, I may go into race car driving professionally."

"I would like to see you drive a race car or—what did you call them? Go-karts?"

I explained the finer points of indoor go-karting to Finn.

"I guess you do have fun." The sheep started to move very slowly. "What else?"

"Um, I think I covered everything." Well, I'd left out hanging out at the Donut Hole, shopping, makeup, and getting mani-pedis and hair done, because I didn't think he'd appreciate those kinds of things.

"What about a boyfriend?"

"I don't have a boyfriend." The road cleared enough for Mrs. Buck to move forward a bit. The car jolted into gear. "Good to know," he said under his breath with his eyes on the fields.

23

❧

Just before noon we returned to the center of the town of Newcastle and got out to walk around. The streets were packed with people. Half wore orange jerseys and waved orange flags and bandannas. The other half wore green and waved green flags and bandannas.

Mrs. Buck found a table and spread out her cards.

Finn and I walked toward the mob. Finn tapped the shoulder of a sweaty guy in an orange shirt. He had mud in his hair and on his legs and arms. "Is the tourney over?"

"Yeah. We won!" he yelled. "We beat da team Dingle. Crushed 'em like a clove of garlic." He sounded like the guy from Wilmington Pizza.

"Ask him about Anna," I whispered.

He heard my accent. "You American?"

"Yeah."

"You like rugby? This is not football, or what you call *soccer*. We play a real sport. You hear of it?"

"Yes," I said. "I've heard of rugby."

"Well, all right!" He held up a high five for me, and I smacked it. "Yeah! Hang out and celebrate. There is plenty of free crisps and soda for everyone!" He was scooped up by teammates and thrust onto their shoulders.

The crowd lifted him and chanted, "Enzo! Enzo!"

I guessed he was Enzo. He called down to me, "I scored da winning goal!"

"Congratulations!" I yelled back. Enzo was carried away into the crowd.

It was really loud with chanting, singing, and music. Finn got close to me and spoke right into my ear. "Looks like fun. Let's hang out. Get a soda?"

"Okay. But we're looking for Anna."

"Got it." Finn went off to grab us something to drink.

I walked around in search of Anna in the huge crowd. Someone stepped on my foot, untying my shoelaces. As I bent down to tie them, someone tripped over my back, and the next thing I knew, Enzo was on the ground next to me.

Someone asked him, "Are you okay?"

Someone else yelled, "Call an ambulance!"

Enzo stood up slowly, rubbed his head and his lower back. "No worries. I'm a tough rugby player." Blood dripped from his hairline.

Finn returned with two Cokes, stopping short when he saw Enzo. "Look what I did," I said. "We have to find Anna O'Toole before something else bad happens."

I was pushed and shoved and found myself among the green team, the ones who'd lost the rugby game, but you'd never know it. They were covered in crusty mud, arm in arm, singing songs of victory. Someone threw an arm over my shoulder and included me in a row of high kicks, which I was good at, but I had to find Anna.

A girl shouldered her way into the team with fists full of warm soft pretzels. She looked a little older than me and was tall and muscular. Her hair was short, the same color and wavy-frizzy as mine. Her eye was swollen, her lip was fat, and drops of dried blood were around her nose. She was *très* muddy. Everyone took a pretzel and patted her on the back.

I asked her, "You played too?"

"Of course. GIRLS RULE!" Her voice was high and

girly. It didn't match her tough and dirty appearance. "Want a pretzel?"

"Sure. Thanks." I took one. "I'm Meghan."

"Hi, Meghan." She took a huge bite of the pretzel. "I'm so hungry." She took mustard packets out of her pocket. "You like mustard?" She opened one and squeezed it into her mouth.

"Sure," I said. "On my pretzel."

She opened another and squeezed it onto both of our pretzels.

Someone in a green shirt called, "Where is our MVP? Where's our most valuable player?"

Another player yelled, "Anna! Where's Anna?"

Anna?

24

∿

The girl with the mustard called back, "Yoo-hoo. I'm over here." She wiggled her fingers and tilted her head in a cute way, which was weird, considering she looked like a boy covered in mud.

This was Anna? I took a closer look. Of course this was Anna! Besides the age and height difference, and the cuts and bruises, it was like I was looking into a mirror.

"There's our girl!" A guy put a ridiculous green-and-white beret on her head. The way her hair stuck out underneath it made her look less like a punching bag and more like a girl.

"Are you Anna O'Toole?"

"That's me. How did you know that? I know I'm popular,

but has word of my reputation reached America already?"

"I don't think so. But I'm sure it will soon," I said. "You know, funny thing, I actually came here looking for you."

"You did? Do you follow rugby? You don't seem the type."

"There's a type?"

"Well, they're usually not American. Sometimes English or Scottish, and they're usually taller."

"Taller?" I didn't think I was short.

She nodded and wiped mustard off her mouth with her arm.

I said, "I was looking for you because of a letter, a chain letter."

"Hey," Anna said. "I got a chain letter too. Not that long ago."

"I know. You sent it to Clare, your cousin."

"That's right. We call her CiCi." She looked surprised. "How did you know that? Wait, are you psychic? Can you put me in touch with my dead granny?"

Maybe Anna had gotten knocked in the head and had a concussion.

"I'm not a psychic," I explained. "I came to talk to you about the letter."

"Right. You know I got good luck from it. That's when I decided to ask if I could be on the team, and they said yes." She smiled, and I noticed that she was missing a front tooth.

"Well, I haven't been so lucky. In fact, I've kinda sorta been, like . . ." How should I say this? . . . "Cursed. I'm cursed."

"Oh, no. That's terrible." She stepped back, shoved the rest of the soft pretzel into her mouth, and used her free hands to pull a ladybug figurine out of her sock. She rubbed it all over herself.

"What are you doing?"

"Warding off bad luck. Why would you bring it here to me? Why? Do you hate me? You don't even know me. I don't want bad luck."

This girl was a wee bit o' the Irish—what's the word?—kooky.

I shook my head. "It's not like it's contagious. I made the mistake of not following the rules of the letter. Plus, I actually kind of do know you, and you kind of know me."

"I think I would know if I knew you. You know what I mean?" Anna rubbed the ladybug on her ears and belly. "People are always trying to unload their bad luck on someone else. Well, not today. I'm on a roll—just played a great game, so you and your curse better back off."

I stepped back a bit. "Ladybugs, huh?"

"Yes. Ladybugs," she snapped. "Now would you mind stepping downwind? I don't want any of your bad luck blowing this way. If I get it on me, I don't know what I'll do." She paused in her ladybug cleansing. "Why didn't you just send the letters like you were supposed to? Maybe you deserve the bad luck if you didn't follow the instructions."

I explained the situation about the election, the rush I was in. She listened to every word at a safe distance from me. "So, I have to find the links of the chain letter. I found my cousin Clare."

"I told you we call her CiCi, and she's *my* cousin, not yours."

"That's the big surprise in all this. She's my cousin too. Which means *we're* cousins."

"*Cousin?* Oh, that's just great. The last thing I want is another cousin."

Ironic that I was dying for another cousin and she didn't want one. "Anyway, I need to double hand-shake with you and then find the person who sent the letter to you."

"I don't want to touch you." She extended her hands

like she was shaking the air. "There's your handshake. Now you need to go away and take your bad luck with you. My cousin Quilly sent me the letter. He doesn't need any more bad luck either. Trust me."

"Quilly? Is Quilly his first name?" At this point she was weirding me out, and I kinda wanted to get away from her too.

"Everyone just calls him Quilly." She poked a teammate. "Hey, what's Quilly's full name?"

She doesn't know her own cousin's real name? I guess being part of a bigger family meant that there were a few crazy relatives. I loved the idea that now *I* had a few crazy relatives! YAY!

He said, "Quilly. It's just Quilly."

I was getting frustrated. How was I going to find this guy without his name?

Another guy was listening, and he said, "Leo . . . er . . . Lem . . . er . . . Lefty . . . er, maybe Ted."

Anna shrugged. She tucked the ladybug back into her sock; reached into her muddy pocket, where another soft pretzel was hiding; and put it into her mouth. "And you say he's your cousin? How is he related to you?"

"Our mothers are sisters. Why?"

I didn't answer. She'd just confirmed Quilly was my cousin too. This was a lot to process.

"Where does Quilly live?"

She stepped farther away from me. "In the city."

My face must've asked, *What city?*

"Dublin. Maybe you've heard of it?"

"Can you be a bit more specific, like maybe a street address?"

"He works as a tour guide on one of those double-decker buses." She inched away and spoke louder. "Listen, Quilly has enough trouble. If you're going to see him, it's very important that you don't give him any of your curse. Not even a little bit." She continued, "Here's what you have to do. Go to Murphy's down the street. Get yourself a ladybug and one for Quilly, too."

Someone bumped Anna from behind and dumped their soda down her back.

She glared at me. "Look at this. I'm drenched in soda!"

Maybe she hadn't noticed that she was covered in mud and everyone else was pretty much wearing soda too?

"You need to leave, and don't come looking for me again." I couldn't believe she was genuinely mad at me because someone else had poured soda on her. She turned away, took the ladybug out again, and rubbed it through her muddy hair.

I was pretty sure she didn't like me. *And* I'd forgotten to invite her to the Spring Fling. Maybe she was going anyway since it was such a big deal. At least I had gotten a lead on Quilly—the second-to-last link—the key to finding the letter's author and ending this whole mess.

I shoved through the crowd looking for Finn. I didn't see him, but my luck started to change when I saw who was sitting next to Mrs. Buck playing Go Fish.

25

❧

"Carissa!" I exclaimed, shocked.

She ran to me and hugged me.

"What are you doing here?" I asked.

"You said everything sucked, and I told you I was coming. Didn't you get the message?"

I laughed. "Yeah, I did. I didn't think you were serious."

"As serious as a monkey is about his last banana." She hugged me again. "Guess where my mom and dad took me for spring break?" She didn't wait long enough for me to answer. "Paris! So, awesome. But when I got your text on our layover in London, we just rerouted to Ireland."

"You're kidding."

"Not even a little bit. Then I called that castle you're

staying at— Hello, castle? Freakin' awesome! They gave me Mrs. Buck's digits because you're not answering your phone. She texted me the deets of your location, and Mom and Dad just dropped me off. Guess where we're gonna stay? Don't—I'll tell you. The castle." She scanned the crowd of rugby players. "This place is awesome! I love Ireland!"

A group of rugby players behind her heard her say this, and cheered. She cheered right back at them, and then they yelled back at her, and she was going to cheer back at them, but I pulled her away. "Stop that," I said.

"What's wrong with a girl having a little fun?" She waved to the group of boys.

"Come on. Boys can wait." I moved her farther away from them. "I'm dealing with a curse here, or did you forget? We have something important to do."

She looked over her shoulder to see if the rugby team was watching her.

With both hands I turned her face back to look at me. "It involves *shopping*," I said.

"Well, why didn't you say so?" she replied. She hooked her arm in mine and asked, "Where to? You name it. Any place you pick is fine by me. Hollister? Justice? Abercrombie? PacSun?"

"Uh-uh," I said.

"Nordstrom?" Carissa asked.

"Murphy's."

"Murphy's?"

"Murphy's."

"I don't know that place. Let's check it out," she said.

I led Carissa down the street to a sidewalk store. The M had dropped into a W, making it look like "Wurphy's." But it was the letter U that signaled to me that this was the place. It was a horseshoe. "Here we are."

Carissa stared. "This? This is the place?" she asked in disgust.

"This is the place where we'll find a lucky ladybug."

"Well, then by golly, we'd better go inside and get a ladybug. When the time is right, you'll explain to me exactly why we're buying insects. I don't want to burst your bubble, but bugs are unlucky. They bite, sting, infest, and carry diseases and poison. But, whatev. You know more about this stuff than I do. Maybe I'll get an ant or a housefly. I've always wanted one of those."

I rolled my eyes. "Stop being so dramatic." I pulled her inside. "And, for your information, neither ants nor houseflies are lucky."

Murphy's smelled like the bottom of a dirty pipe. It looked like one too. The store was filled with antiques and lots of good luck charms. There were four-leaf clovers, horseshoes, angels, rabbit's feet, wishbones, stars, crystals, seashells, sea glass, sand dollars, and ladybugs. Lots of ladybugs.

"Great store." Carissa made a face, held her nose with her fingers, and leaned against a wall with peeling wallpaper.

I studied the case that held all of the ladybug figurines. "Which one should I get?"

"Hmmm. Let me think. Oh, I know . . . I don't care! Just pick one out and let's get the heck out of here." She lowered her voice. "It stinks, and I can't breathe."

"Ahem." An old freckled man asked, "What can I do ya for, lassies?" His voice was low and raspy, like he'd smoked a lot of cigars.

I put a ladybug on the counter. He picked it up and held it close to his eyes. "Excellent choice." He unfolded a piece of soft felt. He put the ladybug figurine that was no bigger than a quarter and no fatter than a raisin into the felt and shined it. He bent down close to me. "You know they're luckiest when they travel in threes," he said, like he was letting me in on a secret, which was just the look that attracted Carissa.

"Three, you say?" she asked. "Why three?"

"Three is a magic number," I explained to Carissa.

"That's right," he said. "I'll do you a hand's turn and give you three for the price of one."

I didn't know what that meant, but it sounded okay.

Carissa asked, "Why is three magical?"

I said, "It just is. You know—burgers, fries, and a shake. The three blind mice. The three little pigs. The three little kittens who lost their mittens—"

"I get it," she said. "You convinced me."

I picked out a ladybug a little bigger and one a little smaller than the original.

"Now let's go see where that rugby team went." Carissa led the way out of Murphy's.

"Or," I said, "let's find Quilly, who is the third link we need."

"The third? Ooooooo. You know, it's a magic number," she teased.

"Stop it," I said. "We need to get Finn and get going." I wondered if there would be something extra lucky about Quilly, since he was third. Maybe something magical was going to happen.

"Quilly, Finn. Finn, Quilly," Carissa said. "There's

something else you need first. Actually, it's important. Possibly more important than a bug, but I'm not going to debate it with you."

"What? Another good luck charm? I'm wearing my clover necklace and I have a rabbit's foot in my pocket. I think I'm covered."

"That's all good," she said. "But that's not what I was talking about. I haven't asked you why you're dressed that way. And I don't care. But I'm here to encourage you to get a new outfit. I don't think you'll get that kind of support from Mrs. Buck. She doesn't look like much of a *Project Runway* gal, if you know what I mean. Capes are so last year."

I looked down at myself and was reminded of the donations I was wearing. "Maybe just a shirt."

"That's all I needed to hear," Carissa said. "Wait here. I'll take care of everything. That's what a bestie is for."

While Carissa went into a shop, I unfolded the soft felt and studied the three ladybugs. Each black spot was painted so nicely, probably by hand. I wondered whose. Less than three minutes had passed when Carissa returned with a cute tank top, hoodie sweatshirt, and tan yoga-type pants. "I outdid myself, I know," she said proudly. "If I were you, I'd put these on now. Like 'Do not pass go, do not collect two hundred dollars' until you change clothes."

I ducked behind a bush and carefully put the tank over the shirt I was wearing and took the other one off underneath and slid it out from under the tank. I pulled the hoodie on. It made me feel like my old self. Then I hid behind a pile of hay and swapped the pants, superfast. "Okay," I said. "Now let's go find Finn."

"Right, Finn. Who's Finn? A boy, I hope."

"Yes. A boy." I wanted to say "And keep your paws off him" but didn't.

I saw him at the edge of the crowd. He seemed like he was looking for me. My wave caught his eyes, and he caught Carissa's.

"*Hellooo*, Finn," Carissa said.

26

Carissa sat in the soup can's front seat next to Mrs. Buck, who had put her gigantic headphones back on. We strapped most of her stuff to the roof and stowed one of her suitcases at my feet, so my knees were pretty much up my nose. The ride to Dublin was filled with the chatter of me giving Carissa all the information of our adventure.

At one point Carissa made a time-out *T* with her hands. "You left in the dark? Totally prepared to run away? Meghan McGlinchey, the girl who has never broken a rule in her life? I'm proud of you."

I smiled.

She said to Finn, "Bravo to you, castle dweller, for encouraging her. You've got a little bad streak in you. I like that."

"Not really *bad*," Finn tried to correct her, blushing.

She was so embarrassing sometimes.

"Usually I have to talk her into stuff," Carissa explained. "Maybe this funny-smelling Irish air has done something to her."

Finn said, "Sounds like you're a good friend. She needs someone to help her break out of her shell a bit, or she'll never have any fun."

"Amen to that," Carissa said.

I saw the signs for Dublin—we were almost there. Suddenly, out of nowhere, a white, fluffy sheep darted out into the road. Mrs. Buck swerved to avoid it and landed us in a ditch that we weren't getting out of.

27

We stood around the soup can and assessed the damage. Not bad, but bad enough. We were stuck.

We only lingered a minute before Finn flagged down a red double-decker tour bus.

I rubbed the ladybug in my palm as the bus stopped. The door opened, and Finn quickly convinced the driver to take us to Dublin.

"Where's the tour guide?" I asked. The driver pointed up to the second level. We were making our way to the stairs when a voice came from the speakers: "Hello, and welcome to Dublin. My name is Sean McCormick, and I'm goin' to share our city with you. You can get on and off this bus at any stop. You just wait for another bus like this one, and with your ticket you can hop back on."

"Let's get off at the next stop," Finn said. "We can hop on and off until we find Quilly."

We agreed.

I saw Mrs. Buck playing a game on a cell phone. "Is that your phone?" I asked Carissa.

"No. It's hers. I just showed her how to download Vintage." Vintage was the hottest new game app.

"Did she ask for your help?"

"Of course. Do you think I read minds?"

"She's supposed to be on a silent retreat."

"That chatterbox? No way," Carissa said.

The woman was talking to everyone but me. I didn't get it. She gritted her teeth at the game.

Finn watched over her shoulder, asking questions about the game. "Who's that guy? Can't you jump?"

Mrs. Buck opened her mouth like she was going to reply, but when she caught sight of me, she zipped her lips.

I sighed in frustration, then said to Carissa, "You know this bus is going to break down, right? Maybe I actually am psychic, because I can predict that this bus will break down, probably on a railroad track, under a rain cloud, and everyone on board will be crushed."

"Where are your bugs? Maybe you should hold them," Carissa said.

I took the other two bugs out of the felt and squeezed them in my fist.

"Try to chill out," Carissa ordered.

I looked out the window at dreary Dublin and tried to chill out. Sean McCormick told us about Molly Malone selling cockles and mussels. There was a statue of her with the cart she pushed around Dublin.

The bus stopped at the famous vampire creator Bram Stoker's house, and that's when we got off.

Sean's bus pulled away.

"See," Finn said. "No train tracks."

Mrs. Buck continued to play her game while we toured the house and learned a lot about Dracula. Most people believed that Stoker invented vampires, but there had been tales of the undead bloodsucking creatures throughout England and Europe for centuries before Stoker. It wasn't my favorite thing, but Carissa was in heaven—she was the biggest vampire fan out there. She asked tons of questions.

When we were done, we waited at the stop for the

next bus. We saw that it was guided by a woman, who was obviously not Quilly. So we let it go and waited for another one.

"If so many cultures from different places around the world at different times in history believed in the undead, they must be real," Carissa declared.

"You're jokin', right?" Finn asked.

Discussion of the undead made me nervous, so I subtly took a ladybug and rubbed it on my head, making it look like I was fluffing my hair or scratching. I made a mental note to get some garlic. Better yet, maybe I could soak the ladybug in minced garlic. I might have just invented a whole new charm to ward off bad luck *and* vampires.

"It's just a folk tale," Finn added. "Monsters aren't real."

"How can you be so sure?" I asked.

"I guess if a letter can bring a curse, then the undead can also be real." I sensed Finn was being sarcastic, but it was tough to tell with his accent.

The arrival of another red bus interrupted the vampire talk. It was guided by a potential Quilly, so we got on. He looked like he was in high school, maybe older, and wore dark sunglasses. The bus company shirt he wore was too tight over muscular arms. He looked like he lifted lots of very heavy things. His hair was light brown and looked like it could use a wash, cut, and brush. But who was I to talk?

Carissa bumped Finn out of the way and sat as close as she could to the guy. "Hey there," she said sweetly.

Finn asked the guy, "Do you know Quilly?"

"I'm working, mate. Can't help you."

Carissa whispered to Finn. "Let me handle this. Watch and learn." She took out a pack of gum, unwrapped a piece for herself, and handed a piece to the guide. "You wanna piece? Your throat probably gets dry from talking all day."

He took it and looked at her over his sunglasses. "Thanks. You American?"

"Yeah. It's Carissa. And that was watermelon flavored."

"I'm Ryan, and I like watermelon."

Ryan? That wasn't anything like Lem, Leo, or Ted. This wasn't our guy.

"Then this is your lucky day," Carissa said to Ryan.

"I'm anything but lucky," he said, and folded the gum into his mouth and talked into the microphone about Dublin City University as we passed by. Then he took a break and asked Carissa how she liked the city.

"So far I love it. It would be even better if I could find my friend Quilly. He works for one of the bus companies. Maybe you know him?"

I waited for Ryan to say it was Quilly's day off, or he'd been fired, or he'd moved away—maybe to Italy or Iceland. Instead his face no longer looked like he was happy to be talking to Carissa. "Whatcha need Quilly for? Does he owe you money?"

"Nah, nothing like that," she said. "Do you know him?"

Ryan announced to the passengers, "We're headed to the country. It's a great place to look for that sheep with a red bow. He could be anywhere." He narrated some more Dublin facts, then asked us again, "Who sent you guys for Quilly?"

"No one sent us," I said. "We just wanted to talk to him."

Ryan continued the tour. "In the mid-1800s Ireland was plagued by a great famine." During his next break he said, "Look, tell whoever sent you that Quilly isn't around."

Finn said, "We just want to talk to him. Do you know where we can find him?"

"No, sorry. I can't help you," he said firmly. "Maybe you should go sit up top till the next stop."

The bus driver slowed down and called back to Ryan,

"Yo, Quilly. You're gonna miss the cliffs. You gonna talk about the cliffs?"

Ryan was Quilly.

Quilly was Ryan.

"You're Quilly?" Carissa asked him. "Why did you pretend you weren't?"

He sighed. "I try to keep a low profile."

"Here." I took out a ladybug. "Anna said I should give this to you."

He took it. "I need all the good luck I can get, but if Anna told you to give this to me, she must've thought you were trouble. Well, I don't want any. You can get off at the next stop. In fact . . ." He called to the driver, "Mate, pull over. They're getting off."

"No," Carissa said to the driver. "He's just kidding; he's a big kidder." Then to Quilly she said, "We don't want any trouble."

I said, "We need to talk to you about the chain letter you sent to Anna."

"We just want to know who sent the letter to you," Finn added.

"If you have to know, it was my dear old granny, Grandma Leona," Quilly snapped. "I sent it because she seemed into it, so I played along. Plus, if that sort of thing is true, I didn't want any trouble, so I sent the letters like I was supposed to. End of story."

Carissa asked, "Do you know where can we find her?"

"I'm a tour guide. I'm like MapQuest without the computer. Of course I know where you can find her. She's at 825 Strand Street, Wicklow. It must be your lucky day, because guess what? We're headed toward Wicklow."

He called to the driver, "Mate, turn right." Then to us he said, "We're on our way. Until then, take your bad luck to the back of the bus."

"Thanks, Quilly," I said. "I mean *cousin*." I raised my eyebrows and smiled.

"I don't have any relatives in the US."

"You do now. Are you ready for this? My dad and your mother are brother and sister. I'm going to introduce them at the Spring Fling. Will you come and bring her?"

"Maybe. If you give me that bug."

"I heard they work better if you pass them off with a double handshake."

"I never heard that."

"It's an American thing."

"Fine." We did the handshake. "Cousins, huh?"

"Yeah."

Quilly pondered this for a moment. "I never had an American cousin before. I guess that's cool."

We were getting off the bus in Wicklow when something hit me. "Did you say 'granny'?"

"Yeah."

"As in grandmother?"

"That's the idea, yeah," Ryan said.

"Is it your mom's mom?"

"That's her, Grandma Leona McGlinchey."

The bus door closed. That was my dad's mother, my grandma Leona McGlinchey. I had a grandmother!

28

Quilly called Wicklow "Viking City." It was breathtaking, with its high rock cliffs and small jagged coves along the coast. Waves of the Irish Sea, probably freezing cold, crashed on the cliffs and coves. Those coves would've been a perfect place for Viking ships to hide.

Strand Street wasn't hard to find, and neither was number 825. I expected a tiny row house with dusty lace curtains, a home in which Grandma Leona would be sitting with a quilt on her lap, drinking tea and doing cross-stitch. Maybe she'd be attached to an oxygen tank. I had a grandmother, and I was about to meet her. I wondered if she'd be able to tell just by looking at me that I was her granddaughter.

Instead of a house we found a grand cathedral. The stone exterior had soaked up the moisture in the air, making it dark gray. There were tall pointy peaks that gave it an eerie Gothic feel.

"Do you think Quilly got the address wrong?" I asked.

"He's like MapQuest, remember?" Carissa said.

Finn walked to the double doors and heaved one open. Before going in, I hopped a pattern: two, one, two, one, one, two. Finn watched but didn't ask me what I was doing and didn't even make a funny face. Mrs. Buck copied me, although she probably had no idea why.

We walked down a red carpet that might have been plush a long, long time ago. Pews lined either side. Mrs. Buck sat down in one and continued her game.

A woman wiped the altar with a rag.

Grandma Leona, at last. The final link.

I could feel the curse lifting already.

She looked exactly like I thought she would: apron, white hair, bifocal glasses. Finally the end of our search and the end of my bad luck. I could tell by looking at her that Quilly's grandma Leona was a kindhearted woman who would give me a double handshake and forgive me. In a matter of seconds the curse would be lifted. The clouds would disappear, and maybe angels would sing.

The woman stopped cleaning and looked at us. She didn't recognize me just yet. "Mass, six o'clock," she said. "Not now." She sounded Spanish or Portuguese. Strange that Grandma Leona wasn't Irish.

I asked, "Are you Quilly's grandma Leona?"

"Mass, six o'clock," she said again.

Carissa whispered, "That's not gonna happen."

I shushed her.

"Thank you," Finn said to the woman. Then to me he said, "I don't think her English is very good."

"Why doesn't Grandma Leona speak English? Isn't that weird? I wonder who wrote the letter for her."

Carissa said, "Um, I don't think this is our gal."

I didn't like the sound of that, because we'd gotten so close. I really thought we'd found her. I thought she'd take away my bad luck right then. But instead I got *this* woman— darn that curse! My shoulders slumped.

Finn said, "I hate to say it, but I think Quilly sent us on a wild grandma chase. He just wanted to get rid of us, so Mr. MapQuest picked some random location and bumped us off the bus."

We left the church and sat on its front steps. Carissa

said, "We should go back and make him tell us where she lives. I'm going to go find a bus schedule." She walked down the street and into a little shop. I knew she was going to come out with more than a bus schedule.

A priest walked down the sidewalk and up the steps. He looked at his watch. "A line already? I knew my Masses were getting popular, but I didn't think there would be a line this early."

We forced smiles.

The priest asked, "You're not here for my Mass, are you?"

Finn said, "Not exactly, Father."

"No?" he asked, disappointed. "Come on anyway. You can tell me what's on your mind. I have some time now."

"Actually," Finn said, "we're lookin' for someone. She's our friend's grandmother. Her name is Leona."

"Oh, yes. Leona. Wonderful woman. Follow me, and I'll show you where she is."

"Really?" I asked. Things started looking better. I would find Grandma Leona and beg her to forgive me and break the curse. Of course she would, and we'd all have tea and scones and talk about what Quilly was like when he was a baby.

I was so deep in thought about Leona that I wasn't paying attention to where we were walking. When I looked up, I saw Finn staring at a tombstone: Leona McGlinchey.

My grandmother. This was her grave.

She was dead.

29

❧

"She just passed away recently," the priest said. "Stay as long as you like." He left us there in the small cemetery behind the church with Leona McGlinchey.

For, like, ten minutes I'd believed I had a grandmother. I stared at her headstone. It was very strange to see the word "McGlinchey" engraved.

I would've loved to have met her. That was the worst luck ever. I was never hopscotching again.

Whether she'd intended to or not, she'd somehow brought me and my family to Ireland to find the rest of our relatives. Her whole family was together because of *her*. It was a shame she wasn't there to enjoy it.

I wiped tears from my eyes.

Finn said, "Maybe there's a stipulation that someone else can forgive you for e-mailing a chain letter? Maybe one of your new aunts."

I shook my head and sat on the ground, leaning against Grandma Leona's tombstone. "I doubt it." I sighed.

"Why didn't Quilly tell us she was dead?" Finn asked, and then he sat next to me like he had in Paddy Flanigan's backyard when we'd played checkers.

"I want to punch Quilly. He could've told us, you know, that she was dead before we came here," I said angrily. "For a little while I actually believed I was going to see her."

After a few minutes of quiet, Finn said, "I think it's kind of cool that she sent that chain letter before she died and it ended up reuniting her children. That's, like, the best luck of all."

"Maybe she should've thought things through, because now she's dead and I'm cursed for life."

"I've been thinking about that," Finn said. "I've been with you for three days now, and you've pointed out how we've had all this bad luck. And maybe some things haven't been great, but look at what you've found."

"Cousins?"

"And aunts and uncles. You have this amazing surprise

for your da. You have, like, the most incredible—what do you say? Bestie?—in the world. She thought you were in trouble and she found you here," Finn said. "Maybe unlucky stuff just happens all on its own. Do you think everyone down on their luck is cursed?"

"Maybe they are and they don't know it," I said.

Finn said, "I guess that's possible." For the first time I noticed the light freckles under his eyes. I pointed to them. "Were these darker when you were a kid?"

"Oh, yeah. I had a lot more of them too."

"Do you miss them?"

"Not really. I never liked them."

"I couldn't have done any of this without you."

"And I wouldn't have had so much fun this week without you. That curse turned out to be very lucky for *me*."

I took my eyes away from Finn's and looked into the distance, where there was something incredible. *Très* epic, as Carissa would say. Over the cliffs of Wicklow was a rainbow.

Then it got even better—it doubled. I wanted to put this moment into a snow globe—well, sans cemetery, dead granny, and cursed-for-life parts—and save it forever.

"I guess we can go back to Castle Ballymore," I said.

"Let's get Carissa and Mrs. Buck and hop on a bus."

"What about the car?" I asked.

"I'll take care of it with Owen and Gene later." He stood up, held his hand out for me, and pulled me up with more muscle than I'd expected. When I stood, I was really close to his face. So close that I thought he might kiss me, but he didn't. He took my hand and led me to the sidewalk and down a street in Wicklow.

Could he be looking for a more perfect place to kiss me?

Could there be anything better than a double rainbow back-drop?

Maybe a fountain with little fairies surrounding us with flowers and twinkle lights?

We stopped at the church. Finn went in to get Mrs. Buck while I went to the little shop to get Carissa, who had bought T-shirts for all of us that said KISS ME I'M IRISH.

"I'm starving," Carissa said as Finn and Mrs. Buck were coming out of the church.

In response to that comment, Mrs. Buck clapped to get our attention. (As if I didn't know she'd been selectively talking this whole time.) Then she pointed to her open mouth. She was hungry too.

"That lady is a hoot," Carissa said, and copied the *I'm hungry* motion as if Mrs. Buck was a real jokester.

Finn said, "I'll never turn down a burger." We followed him down the street to a pub. He held the door open for me and led us to a booth with worn red leather seats and a sticky table.

Carissa and I ordered Cokes with ice and french fries, extra well done. Finn ordered burgers for himself and Mrs. Buck.

"So, what happened?" Carissa asked.

"She's dead," I replied. "Grandma Leona was nothing more than a tombstone."

"What are you gonna do?" Carissa asked.

"I guess I could wrap myself in bubble wrap and stay away from people for the rest of my life," I said.

Mrs. Buck nodded in agreement.

Carissa slurped the bottom of her Coke. "I'm gonna tell you something, but you have to promise not to get mad."

I narrowed my eyes at her. "What?"

"Remember the day we were in the bathroom stall together?" She looked at Mrs. Buck. "Only place we could have privacy," she explained. Mrs. Buck nodded and took a huge bite of her burger.

"Yup," I said. "That day is imprinted on my brain forever, even though I've tried to forget it."

"So," she started. "Actually, you might find this funny. It's funny when you think about it." She bit a fry.

Somehow I didn't think I was going to find this funny.

"You know how we were looking up chain letter stuff on my phone and I told you what you needed to do to undo the bad luck?"

"Yeah," I said. "I kinda remember that clearly because that's why we're all here."

"Totally." She nervously put another fry into her mouth. "You see, the thing is . . ."

"What?" I yelled. Mrs. Buck jumped.

In one breath Carissa said, "I sorta kinda made some of that up."

"You *what*? How much did you 'sorta kinda' make up?" I yelled.

"Sorta kinda all of it." She pushed more fries into her mouth.

30

I told Carissa I wasn't talking to her. But that didn't stop her from talking to me. Mostly she said, "I'm sorry."

We waited at the Wicklow bus stop and let several buses pass because I wanted Quilly's bus. He was going to feel the wrath of Meghan McGlinchey, who was now in a very bad mood.

The sun began to set. Finn said, "I think we should take the next bus, or we might be stuck here all night. They stop running eventually."

"Don't even," I said, holding up my hand. "I *am* going to see Quilly tonight."

"But it doesn't matter if none of this reversal stuff was true in the first place," Finn argued.

"It matters to me."

A bus approached with its lights on. I knew we'd have to take it whether it was Quilly's or not.

The door opened, and I recognized the driver. Someone behind him yelled, "We're full." It was Quilly.

We got on anyway. The bus was mostly empty.

I sat close to him and wasted no time letting him know what I felt. "You could've told us she was *dead*." I refrained from punching him in the nose and calling him a moron. He didn't offer an explanation, and he didn't talk to me.

I was too tired to yell at him anymore. I'd made my point.

Carissa and I stared at the patchwork-quilted country-side slowly turning gray in the sunset.

That's when I saw it. At first it was just a flash of color. Then it became more clear. I elbowed Finn and yelled, "The ribbon! It's the red ribbon! The sheep with a red bow! Over there! I found it!"

Carissa asked, "What ribbon?"

I ignored her.

Finn yelled, "Stop the bus!"

Everyone shifted to our side of the bus and looked out

the window. Carissa asked the entire bus, "What ribbon?" No one answered. They were all too excited looking at the field.

The bus stopped, and I ran out, Finn right behind me. I heard Carissa say, "I'll stay here."

I think Mrs. Buck said "Me too," but I didn't turn around to check.

I slowed as I got closer. I thought I might scare him away, but I didn't. He was all alone, bent over chomping on damp grass.

"Hey there, buddy," I said calmly and sweetly. "Let me get that pesky bow off your neck for you." I pulled the bow's velvety tail. It untied easily in my hand. I waved it over my head. Everyone on the bus cheered, including Carissa, who apparently had gotten the details from someone, probably Mrs. Buck, who was secretly talking again.

I leapt toward Finn and hugged him. I did. And it felt so good—*parfait*, in fact.

When we got back on the bus, Quilly had already called someone at the Spring Fling's headquarters from the bus radio and was explaining what had happened. He let go of the radio button. "They need your name."

"Meghan McGlinchey."

He pressed the button. "Meghan McGl—" He let go of the button again. "Did you say 'McGlinchey'?"

"Yeah. Why?"

"That was my grandma's last name. I guess we really are cousins."

Quilly pushed the radio button in and finished giving my information to the person at the other end of the line. "You're all set for Friday," he said to me.

Carissa asked, "Dare I ask what Friday is?"

Finn answered, "It's the Spring Fling, and now Meghan is the official hostess."

"This really is your lucky day," Carissa said, forgetting that I wasn't talking to her. I didn't reply. "I don't know how you can be mad at me when all of this great stuff is happening to you because of the little teeny tiny lie I told you. You know, you should thank me."

Should I? I would be the hostess of the celebration. Once I told my dad what I'd discovered, I would be the hero of my family too.

Maybe Carissa was right. I'd found cousins, a grandmother (even though she was gone), the sheep with the bow, Owen, Gene, and Finn. Finn.

Carissa pried Mrs. Buck's phone away from her. She

looked at the screen of the game. "Quite impressive, you freaky cape-wearing gamer."

Mrs. Buck was clearly just about to say something, but then changed her mind.

Carissa took a picture of all of us with the red bow.

"So," Finn said. "Do you still think you're cursed?"

Could it have been that somehow over the last two days the curse had lifted?

31

I was thrilled at the sight that greeted me at the castle doors.

Piper stood on top of a mountain of suitcases. "Our luggage!" Then she saw me. "Meghan's back! And Carissa! And FINN! EVERYONE! MEGHAN'S BACK!" She took a deep breath in preparation for yelling louder. "EVVEERRRY–"

"We're here," Dad said, and helped her climb off the mountain. "You're back," he said, and hugged me. "How was your expedition and night at Mrs. Buck's brother's?"

"In a word," I said, "eventful."

Owen came in and guided me to the parlor, where Gene was serving tea. "Do come in and tell us all about it."

Everyone was there. Mom held Hope near the fire, Shannon sat with her foot extended, Mr. Leary delivered scones on fancy plates to the silent ladies, Carissa's mom and dad sat in matching Queen Anne chairs sipping from dainty teacups, and Eryn's nose was glued to her phone.

"There's so much to tell you that I'm not sure where to start," I said.

"How about the curse," Finn suggested to me under his breath when he handed me a scone.

"That's good," I said. "I'm not cursed anymore! At least I'm pretty sure. There's one little detail that still needs to be worked out, but generally speaking, I'm not cursed anymore."

"Hallelujah," Piper chanted. "Can somebody gimme an 'amen'?"

No one did.

Shannon asked, "How'd you manage that?"

"Well, actually, I did what Piper said."

"That's right! It was my idea. Generally speaking, you all don't think that I have good ideas, but I DO!"

Dad put his hand on her shoulder. "Of course you do. Let's let Meghan finish."

"I found one link, which led me to another and another

and another. They all—pretty much—double hand-shook me and forgave me."

"That is good news," Mr. Leary said.

"Grand," Owen said.

"The grandest," Gene added.

"But wait. There's more," Carissa announced. I'd decided somewhere between Wicklow and Ballymore that I was talking to her again.

I held up the red velvet ribbon. The silent ladies gasped.

"Is it?" Gene asked.

"Can it be?" Owen asked.

"What?" Mom asked. "What is it?"

Mr. Leary said, "I think it is the biggest honor in all the land. Is it?"

I nodded with a big smile and let Mr. Leary explain to my family and Carissa's the significance of the red ribbon.

Shannon asked, "You're the host of the whole entire festival?"

"Looks that way."

Eryn let out a *Pfft* of annoyance.

"Indeed," Mr. Leary said. "The curse is lifted despite whatever loose end you referred to earlier. No one who finds the red ribbon could be even a little bit cursed."

"Not a smidgen," Owen said.

"Not even a pigeon!" Gene added, and the two twins laughed at themselves.

Mr. Leary said, "This calls for a special meal. Why don't you rest and unpack your very own luggage, and we'll eat at eleven o'clock. It's late, but who cares? Any time is perfect to share a good meal with friends."

"Sounds like you just suggested a nap. And I like naps," Carissa said. "You don't have to ask me twice."

I went to retrieve my luggage from the pile, with help from Gene. I was carrying my suitcase up the dark wood stairs when I said, "You know, I was thinking that maybe you should put this suitcase in your donation closet."

"Why?" Gene asked.

"There's nothing in here that I really need. Besides, now that Carissa is here, she can share her stuff with me."

Everyone in the parlor stared at me. They didn't say anything, but I knew what they were all thinking. "Stop it," I said to them. "I can go shopping when I get home."

My dad came to the foyer and kissed me on the top of my head. Mrs. Buck gave me a thumbs-up.

"If I give them my stuff, can I go shopping when we get

home?" Piper asked. "I can be nice too. Carissa, will you share with me too?"

"I guess," Carissa said reluctantly.

We all looked to Eryn to see what she would do. She shook her head and returned to her silence. It was a refreshing change that I was hoping would be annual, if not monthly.

32

It was still dark when Finn whispered into my ear, "You ready?"

Is this déjà vu?

"We don't have to sneak away this time," I said. "Everyone is going to Spring Fling."

"It starts now," he said.

"It's night."

"I know. Isn't it great? We all hike up the hill to welcome the sunrise."

Carissa, who was next to me in the saggy twin bed, said, "He's quite the joker."

"I am a pretty good joker, but I'm serious about this."

"Why?" Carissa asked. "I thought the Spring Fling was

supposed to be fun. Waking up and hiking in the dark is *not* fun. Trust me."

A shoe sailed across the room at Finn and hit him in the back. "Ouch!"

"Shut up," Eryn growled.

"She's a nasty one. Let her sleep. She doesn't seem like she's Spring Fling material," Carissa said.

"Ouch!" A second shoe hit him.

"I'll see you downstairs," Finn said to us. "We'll find you some boots."

We dressed in Carissa's clothes in the dark, to avoid getting things thrown at us.

She had really nice clothes, and it felt good to dress in style again.

The boots Finn gave us to use un-styled our outfits a bit.

Finn gave us each a hat. "It's nippy out there. You'll need these till the sun comes out." He put fur-lined hats—trooper style that came over the ears and tied under the chin—on our heads. Besides my rabbit's foot, I'd never touched real fur. "Muskrat," he said. "Da shot it himself."

Ewwww!

More than gross, now the outfit had really lost style.

We set out in the dark with the retreaters, the McGlincheys

(sans Eryn), Carissa's parents, and the other castle dwellers (two of them had Shannon in a wagon) hiking up the hill in the dark to greet spring.

Soon the hike warmed me up. And the hat and the boots, albeit fashion faux pas, worked.

Owen and Gene arrived first and set up a tarp with chairs and blankets for us. The sun rose over the patchwork of green fields that glistened with dew. The sun was strong and bright and warmed us enough that we could lose the hats. Mine had given me enough static to make my hair stand up like in a science experiment.

Soon people started playing fiddles, and tables of vendors selling food, drinks, and crafts opened for business.

A familiar-looking girl walked around with pretzels on a long stick. "Are you still avoiding me?" I yelled to Anna.

"Are you still cursed?" she yelled back.

"Do I look cursed?" I held up the red ribbon.

Anna grinned. "Guess not." We walked closer together, and I could see that her bruises had turned greenish.

I asked, "Is your mom here somewhere?"

Anna pointed to a woman at a table selling handmade sweaters. She was sipping a mug of something steamy. Two other women worked the cash box. "There she is with Aunt Mary and Aunt Colleen."

"Do they know about the surprise?"

"CiCi explained everything."

"Did someone say surprise?" CiCi walked up behind me and wrapped her arms around my waist in a hug. Then she did the same to Carissa. "Is this one of your sisters?"

"No. This is my bestie, Carissa." CiCi hugged her again.

"She looks like she could be a McGlinchey. Doesn't she, Anna?"

"Sure." Anna squeezed a packet of mustard onto a pretzel and bit off a huge piece.

"I need to find Quilly," I said.

"I don't think he'll come to something like this," CiCi said. "He has issues with public places."

"Oh, no," I said. "We need him."

"Tell you what," Anna said. "I'll call him. I know exactly what to say."

"Thanks." Before I walked away, I asked her, "Do you have any extra mustard for my friend?"

"Sure. Sure I do." She handed Carissa three packets. "You're okay," she said to Carissa.

Carissa took the mustard. Under her breath she asked, "Why do I want mustard packets?"

Quietly I said to her, "Just say thank you."

"Thanks!" Carissa exclaimed. "I love mustard!"

"Who doesn't?" Anna asked, and she slapped Carissa hard on the back, making her wince.

We left Anna and CiCi, and I walked right into a familiar-looking woman who was attached to a big wooden tray.

33

"Honey!" It was the woman I'd been certain had been planning to bake me in her oven but instead had rescued us with a tractor. She'd tied a wooden tray to herself with straps around her waist and neck. It was covered with soda bread.

"Oh, m'dear Meghan. How are you? How did you do on your search for those people?"

"So much better than I ever hoped."

"I'm glad for ye." She tried to reach into the pocket of her apron, which was difficult because of the tray on her stomach. "I have your gadget. It's in my pocket. Can you reach it?"

"My phone! Oh, yay! I really missed it."

"I was going to try to call you on it, but I couldn't figure it out." I was so happy to have it back. She also gave us each a loaf of soda bread.

As we walked away Carissa said, "She was nice."

"Yeah. After I figured out that she wasn't going to eat me, then I liked her."

"What?"

"Long story."

In the distance we heard someone yelling, "Ah! Ey! Oy!" And then something flew into the air.

"Let's check that out," Carissa said.

It was pizza dough being tossed high and made into a flat circle. "I know him!" I exclaimed.

"You seem to know everyone," Carissa said admiringly. "You had a busy couple of days without me."

When Enzo saw me, he called out, "American girl!"

I waved and went over to his table.

"You wanna try my pizza?"

"Sure," I said. He put a slice on a plate for Carissa and me.

"I hear that the hostess today is an American. Maybe someone you know?"

"Well, I don't know everyone in America. But I happen to know *that* person very well," I said with a smile.

Just then there was a *tap, tap, tap* on the microphone. A man in a tall green-and-white *Cat in the Hat*–style hat stood in front of everyone. "Excuse me." His words bounced all over the top of the hill. "It's time for the celebration to begin. It's my pleasure to announce this year's lucky hostess—all the way from the USA—from Wilmington, Delaware. Miss Meghan McGlinchey."

Everyone clapped for *moi*. I hadn't really prepared a speech for this, but I stepped up anyway. I looked out at all the people in the crowd who stared, waiting for me to say something. Owen and Gene clapped and whistled. Carissa and Finn stood at my side.

I said, "I've had a great time in your country over the last few days. I met new and wonderful friends that shared so much with me, so thank you all very much." Everyone was listening—nothing like the school gym. "My father came to Ireland to meet his sister Colleen for the first time here today at this Spring Fling. But I have a very, very big surprise for him."

I watched his face redden and his mouth gape open.

"Dad, this is your sister Colleen." I pointed to the woman at the table. She approached him, and they embraced. Everyone at the top of the hill clapped. "But there's more."

Colleen and Dad let go of each other. "You also have a sister Elizabeth and a sister Mary." The other women at the table approached Dad and smothered him in hugs. The hill clapped and clapped more. Tears rolled down Dad's face. "And all these people over here, Dad"—I pointed to a group of twelve kids and three men—"these are your twelve new nieces and nephews, and three new brothers-in-law." The crowd exploded in applause the way that I'd imagined the school gym would with my election speech. "I wouldn't have found these people if it hadn't been for the kindness of all the strangers I met over the last few days. Thank you, Ireland. And welcome, spring!"

CiCi and her dancing friends must have known that was their cue, because they began to jig on a rolled-out wooden floor.

Quilly grabbed my arm as I stepped down from the podium. "Nice speech." He handed me a pair of hard-soled Irish shoes. "Put these on. I'm deliverin' you to the floor."

"I don't think so," I said shyly.

"You want to do it the hard way?" He peered over the top of his sunglasses.

"No." I put the shoes on and followed him to the tapping sound.

CiCi saw me and said, "Come on, come on, come on." She pulled me into line with the girls, and when they stomped, I stomped. Before I knew it, I was kicking in step. Everyone clapped and cheered. The retreaters—now liberated—were the loudest of all. I looked up and smiled at all of my new friends and family who watched me dance.

We stayed at the Spring Fling all day. Eventually, probably out of hunger, Eryn made it to the top of the hill. CiCi ran over to her. "Wait! Are you *another* sister? You look just like the McGlincheys." She hugged Eryn, who really didn't like to be touched. "You know, I think people get grumpy when they're hungry. Come on!" CiCi dragged her away. "You need to meet Paddy Flanigan. He makes the very best cookies."

My dad was spoiled by three older sisters who had missed nurturing him through his childhood. I'd never seen him so happy. Aunt Elizabeth and Aunt Mary took the baby for the whole day, and my mom was finally able to jig a little herself. At one point Dad mouthed "Thank you" to me from afar. He didn't say I was his favorite daughter, but he probably thought it.

After a full day of dancing and celebrating, we eventually hiked down the hill and toppled into our saggy castle beds.

34

Saying good-bye to Castle Ballymore was tough. Saying good-bye to the people in Castle Ballymore was really, really tough.

"I'm going to miss you guys," I said to Owen and Gene. They smothered me in their burlap-smelling hugs. Both of them cried. They hugged Shannon even longer and harder than they had me. They pecked Carissa and Piper on each cheek and hesitantly patted Eryn on the back.

My whole family and Carissa got into the airport shuttle. We found Carissa's parents already waiting for us at the airport.

"I'll e-mail you," I said to Finn.

"And I'll e-mail you back," he said. "I'm so glad I met you, Meghan."

"Me too," I said. He held my hand between both of his for just a second. I thought he might kiss me, but I guess this wasn't my lucky day.

Before getting into the shuttle, I gave him a ladybug. "Just in case luck is real, I want you to have some of it. I have one too. They come in threes. And, well, Quilly has the third one, which is a little weird, but don't pay attention to that part."

"Thanks." Finn smiled.

The shuttle drove away down the narrow, bending road, past the low rock walls and the fields of green speckled with white fluffy sheep. I glanced back and waved one last good-bye.

35

⚭

Six months later

Saint Anthony's feast day was a big deal in Wilmington.

Americans didn't celebrate with festivals, street parties, or random jams the way the Irish did. I had been in full-scale party withdrawal since returning home, so I counted the days until this Italian festival.

It took up four square city blocks and was an amazing display of homemade Italian cuisine, from antipasto to ziti. Singers, dancers, and comedians occupied the many stages. There were rides, carnival games, and parades.

This year it would be even more spectacular because we'd rented a section of the piazza for a party—a McGlinchey family reunion. My dad sat around a table with his three sisters. They looked at pictures, shared stories, and laughed. You could see the resemblance among them in the way they looked and moved. Even after years and oceans apart, they were family.

My cousins were there too. They all waited in line with Carissa, Piper, and me for our favorite ride, the Cliffhanger. On this ride, you lay on your belly, and the machine lifted you up and flew you around like you were Superman. I loved it because I could see the whole Saint Anthony's feast day event from up high, with the backdrop of Wilmington's Little Italy. It was nothing like Dublin. It was home.

The Cliffhanger lifted me, and I began to fly, totally free, with the mid-Atlantic summer wind in my curls. Carissa and I held hands until the wind was too strong. My screams caught on the air and sailed away, maybe over the ocean, maybe all the way to Castle Ballymore, to Finn.

From up there I could also see the dunk tank that the student council from my school had donated. Each year the class president chose the color that we painted the tank. This year I'd chosen green. That's right. I'd become class president. Carissa had demanded a recount when a fistful of ballots had mysteriously turned up under a rock in the school courtyard.

BLING!

Someone had nailed the bull's-eye, and Avery Brown splashed into the tank.

Finn.

Not a day had gone by when I hadn't thought of him.

As I flew through the air, I scanned the crowd below, wishing he was here too.

Suddenly I saw a flash of sandy blond hair.

Could it be?

When the ride ended, I ran ahead of Carissa. "Hey," she shouted after me. "You gonna barf?"

I ignored her and kept running.

"Finn?"

The guy turned.

It wasn't him.

"Sorry," I apologized. "I thought you were someone else."

Carissa caught up. "What's up with you? Where are you going?"

"I thought I saw him," I said.

"Him? Finn? Again?"

"Yeah. But I was sure this time."

A familiar voice from behind me said, "Well, would you look at the time? It's 12:10."

I turned and saw Finn. He was dressed like an ordinary guy in cargo shorts, a white T-shirt, and sandals.

I stepped closer. "It really is you."

Carissa said, "Hello, castle dweller."

I gave her a look that said, *Scram.*

"Jeez," she said, backing up. "I'm going."

"I didn't expect to see you," I said, turning back to Finn.

"Surprise!"

I laughed. "Good one."

The band behind us started playing the newest hit from The Warehouse Boys.

"I love this song!" Carissa yelled. She started dancing around. The crowd grew louder with the music.

I leaned into Finn. "It's really good to see you."

He took my hand. "I had to come here to ask you something that I didn't get a chance to in Ireland."

The fountain next to us turned on, spraying water high into the air. Then a thousand little white twinkly lights wrapped around floral garland turned on. It looked like fairies carrying flowers.

"What?"

"Do you still think that letter was bad luck?"

Then I had the best snow globe moment yet: Finn took my chin in his hands, closed his eyes, and gently touched his lips to mine. He held me tight. It was—how can I explain this?—awesome!

Maybe that letter was pretty lucky after all.

Pack your bags and get
ready for another adventure!

I'm a totally normal thirteen-year-old girl. For real.

The problem is that I'm surrounded by weird.

Dad said, "Come look at this one, Ginger."

He was talking to me. I'm Ginger. I was named after one of my mother's favorite old movie stars, a lady named Ginger Rogers. (Mom is totally obsessed with old movies.)

I walked over to see my dad's latest contraption; he loves to try and make new things out of stuff around the house.

I looked at this Saturday's gizmo. "What is it?"

"I call it the Drool-O-Dabbler."

"Uh-huh." He had taken the plastic chin strap off my

little brother's football helmet. FYI, Grant—who's also named after an old movie star—doesn't use the helmet for football. He tapes balls of aluminum foil to it to help him connect with aliens that might try to talk to him. Although they never actually have; he does it "just in case."

I told ya—surrounded by weird.

Anyway, Dad took the chin strap and melted it to pipe cleaners that he'd bent like candy canes. Then he stuffed the cup of the chin strap with wads of gauze, like from a first-aid kit.

Dad hooked the pipe cleaners over his ears. "You can wear this to soak up your drool while you sleep. Or, I suppose, while you're awake, if you're the kind of person who drools when you're awake. I would imagine there are people like that. And it keeps your pillowcase dry—or your shirt, if you're awake."

"I guess it would come with extra gauze pads," I pointed out.

"Replacements? Sure."

"It's . . . ah . . . great, Dad. This could be TBO." He was always looking for TBO—The Big One. While I agreed there might be people who drool a lot in their sleep—and maybe even some when awake—I wasn't convinced this was TBO, but it always made my dad smile when I told him that.

"I'm gonna need you for the video."

"Of course." I was always in the video. Usually my part was to say, "You know what you need?" Then I would say to someone, usually a part played by Grant, "You need a Drool-O-Dabbler."

Grant would ask, "A Drool-O-Dabbler? What's that?" Then my dad would introduce the product, and a staged bidding war would begin. Well, "war" is a bit of an exaggeration. The highest bidder buys the Dabbler. The craziest part is, there are always people who really want his stuff.

"Just let me know when we start filming," I said, and went to let Grant know about our next acting gig.

I knocked and opened his bedroom door. Until just recently, *his* room used to be *our* room, which was wrapped in posters of UFOs and extraterrestrials. I just had to get out of there. My new room is very pink and neat. I picked out every single thing in it: lamp, curtains, beanbag chair, etc. . . .

"Greetings, earthling," he said.

I rolled my eyes. Some girls have brothers who burp; some have brothers who punch them. I have one who thinks he's parked at my house temporarily while he's in between intergalactic voyages.

Yay me!

Payton and I have said that Grant will be our first patient.

Payton, BTW, is my BFF and future business partner— we're going to be brain surgeons.

"You're needed for an Internet video later," I said.

"I comprehend."

"No duh. Not like it was complicated," I said. I didn't know if Grant actually had a shortage of brain cells or if he had some type of cerebral condition that contributed to his whack-a-doodle behavior. I was about to harass him more, when the phone rang. I ran to the kitchen to grab it.

"Hello. This is Ginger Carlson," I said. One day I would have someone who would answer the phone for Payton and me, "Hello. Dr. Ginger Carlson and Dr. Payton Paterson's office."

"Hello. My name is Leo. I'm Betty-Jean Bergan's house-keeper. Can I talk to you about her?"

This guy thought I was my mom. Probably because I sound so mature. People always told me that.

"Uh—" I tried to interrupt, but didn't succeed.

"Your aunt has had another incident. It was serious. Dude, I don't know what to do about her."

I asked, "What do you mean, *another* incident?" *And why is he calling me (or my mom) "dude"?*

"Oh, my bad. I thought your hubs told you. I spoke to him the other day . . . about her behavior. It's strange. Odd. Halloween without the candy. And today, well . . . she fell."

I gasped. "Is she okay?"

"Get this, she wanted to climb the Hollywood sign," Leo the housekeeper said.

"*THE* Hollywood sign? The big famous one?"

My mom's aunt Betty-Jean (or ABJ, as I call her) lives in Hollywood, California. She's my coolest relative: she's beautiful, used to be an actress, and lives this totally glam life in Hollywood. I've always wanted to visit her, but she comes here instead of us going there. At least, she used to; it's been about three years since I've seen her. Although I don't understand why she would want to come to Delaware when she lives in California.

"There's only one Hollywood sign," Leo continued. "She's out of the hospital, and they said she's gonna be okeydokey, hunky-dory, A-OK, but there's something else. A sitch."

"What kind of sitch?" I asked.

"The money kind. She has none. Zip. Zero. Piggy bank empty." He paused. "The bank wants to take away her house."

I gasped again. "That's terrible!"

"You're telling me. She asked that I call you to see if the family would come out here and help her."

Out there? As in Hollywood? For real? Obvs I want to go to LA, and my mom, the classic movie nut, would totally love it. Dad always says he has to work, but if ABJ needs him, I bet he'd take time off. I mean, he finds time to make contraptions, right?

"I hope you do come, because she doesn't owe money only to the bank."

I covered the mouthpiece and yelled to Mom and Dad in the living room, "ABJ's housekeeper is on the phone. He says that she fell off the Hollywood sign! The bank is taking her house! So we need to go to Los Angeles to help her! Can Payton come? Next week is spring break!"

Mom rushed away from the TV—something she only does for a pee emergency or a grease fire. "Let me have that.

And please stop yelling." She snatched the phone. "Hi, sorry about that. Okay. Uh-huh. Uh-huh. Yes. We'll be there." She hung up. Now Dad and Grant joined us in the kitchen.

Mom said, "My aunt Betty-Jean needs our help. Get ready to go to Hollywood!"

Get lost in these international adventures!

Learn more at aladdinmix.com!

EBOOK EDITIONS ALSO AVAILABLE

From Aladdin   KIDS.SimonandSchuster.com

IF YOU ♥ THIS BOOK,
you'll love all the rest from

YOUR HOME AWAY FROM HOME:

AladdinMix.com

HERE YOU'LL GET:

- ♥ The first look at new releases

- ♥ Chapter excerpts from all the Aladdin M!X books

- ♥ Videos of your fave authors being interviewed

Aladdin ♥ Simon & Schuster Children's Publishing ♥ KIDS.SimonandSchuster.com

Check out these great titles from Aladdin M!X:

ALADDINMIX.COM

EBOOK EDITIONS ALSO AVAILABLE

 | From Aladdin | KIDS.SimonandSchuster.com

Aladdin M!X
Collect them all!

**DOWNLOAD A COMPLETE M!X CHECKLIST
AT ALADDINMIX.COM.**

EBOOK EDITIONS ALSO AVAILABLE

m!x | FROM ALADDIN | KIDS.SIMONANDSCHUSTER.COM

Did you LOVE reading this book?

Visit the Whyville...

Where you can:

- Discover great books!
- Meet new friends!
- Read exclusive sneak peeks and more!

Log on to visit now!
bookhive.whyville.net